D0699227

THE STERILE CUCKOO

THE STERILE CUCKOO

by

JOHN NICHOLS

DAVID McKAY COMPANY, INC.

New York

THE STERILE CUCKOO

COPYRIGHT © 1965 BY JOHN NICHOLS

All rights reserved, including the right to reproduce
this book, or parts thereof, in any form, except for
the inclusion of brief quotations in a review.

This is a work of fiction. Any resemblance of the
characters to persons living or dead is purely coin-
cidental.

The lines from "Grass," by Carl Sandburg, appear
in *Cornhuskers,* © 1918 by Holt, Rinehart and
Winston, Inc., © renewed 1946 by Carl Sandburg;
reprinted by permission of Holt, Rinehart and
Winston, Inc.

MANUFACTURED IN THE UNITED STATES OF AMERICA

To ALAN

In memory of the squash ball, the Dead Bugs, the Jest-No's, and all other Magnificent Frustrations we so soulfully endured.

THE STERILE CUCKOO

CHAPTER ONE

Several years ago, during the spring semester of my junior year in college, as an alternative to either deserting or marrying a girl, I signed a suicide pact with her. This historic event occurred the morning after too many Tiki Puka Pukas the night before had led to too many bandaids, and, amid the gardenias and old cigarette butts, we had had a curiously stunted quarrel.

The girl's name was Pookie Adams: I met her on a bus the summer before I was to enter college. She fell immediately head over heels in love with me, and myself?—I couldn't have cared less about the whole thing one way or another. Which only goes to show not only was I very shy at the time, but a liar as well.

I was sitting on a concrete do-dad in front of the depot restaurant during a supper break in Friarsburg, Oklahoma. The time must have been around six P.M. The sky had been an undecided color for half an hour, then it got dark in a snap and I hunched up and smoked a cigarette down to the nub. Pookie came in on the nub: she sauntered out of the restaurant, a skinny, scrubby-haired, dark-eyed, pale girl, with a thin-lipped sarcastic, almost-smiling mouth, balancing a toothpick on her tongue. Saluting me with a big "Hi-Ho," she sat down on another do-dad several feet away. Before I could catch my breath, she managed to say more mixed-up things than, up until that time, I had heard collectively in my life.

"You're a kind of shaggy, scruffy-looking, bag of bones —the real cowboy role—aren't you?" she began. "And judging from the intense expression on your incredibly boyish face, you are thinking of either punching a gorgeous naked broad in her big white belly, or else catching a flock of tame canaries in a huge net just before they fall into the Mississippi river. All the same, you don't look bad to me, you know. You look like a grown up version of The Kid in the Charlie Chaplin movie, ever see it? Charlie Chaplin movies get me right here, especially 'The Kid,' and more especially when everybody is an angel with paper wings, jerking back and forth on wires you can almost-but-not-quite see. After 'The Gold Rush' I bought some Brown and Serve Rolls, raided a couple of forks from the silverware cabinet in the dining room, and went upstairs to my room where I tried—on my pillow and without much success—to do the dance the way he did it. I love Charlie Chaplin...do you?" When I stared at her exactly as if she were nuts, she said; "I'm not a pushmi-pullyu, I don't have a goiter, nor am I a dyed-in-the-wool Kulack-killing Communist. I'm a girl. Going home," she tacked on with a pout, retreating her hands up out of sight into the shaggy sleeves of her grey sweater.

What was I supposed to do? To say? I leaned over and scooped up a handful of gravel which I began to throw, pebble by pebble, in the direction of the Greyhound parked a few yards away.

[2]

"Where you from?" she asked pertly, gloominess certainly not one of her more prominent traits. I failed to answer right away, and she continued with; "Sorry, I hadn't noticed there was a key stabbed in your back. If I give it a hearty twist do you start talking, dancing, doing push-ups, or what?"

"I'm from New York."

"City?"

"Yeah."

"Imagine that. I've never been east of the Tadpole Pond. You know what I think of as New York? In the foreground is a dashing gay boy in tails, very formal, and on his arm is a round-faced pretty girl wrapped loosely in glistening pale blue satin. Both of them are smoking filtered cigarettes—in black ivory holders, of course. Behind them is the silhouette of a horse-drawn— what are they called . . . hacks?—and standing in front of the horse is a top-hatted-and-tailed driver—coachman, rather—holding his whip stiffly vertical in front of him. In the far far background is the beautiful austere skyline. It's a very cool city, isn't it, with lots of colored marbles, and buildings so high you can look down on the clouds?"

I told her, very concisely, what I, having lived there all my life, thought of New York City. It hardly threw her, because she started right in on her home town, a little heap called Merritt, somewhere in Indiana. This led to a fast, unabashed summary of her life up to the present.

It seems she was a pretty lonely kid who once had a spider in the backyard evergreen tree for a friend, and one day she saved its life by yanking a praying mantis out of its web and throwing the mantis into the open cess-

[3]

pool where some rubber-suited zombies with a Roto-Rooter (or its forefather) were fiddling, all on account of the toilet overflowing in the cellar beside the laundry room because she had tried to flush down a pair of her dirty panties. She terminated this warm friendship on a gloomy note, knocking her spider friend into the grass and squashing him beneath her grubby sneaker, though afterwards she relented and with her finger drew an enchantment circle around the little yellow mess that used to be him. Her eyes tightly closed, she had actually heard a shish in the air—his spirit rising—then all was still: not a flutter of air; nor a scrape of grass; nor a hum of nothing.

Skinny ("Hell, I was downright emaciated..."), knobby as a stick, she had always been happily-go-miserably abnormal, having been, as an only child, one of those lonely little prodigies who went through the rheumatic fever-weak heart-no athletics bit, and she played the role to the hilt, operating out of the Tadpole Pond (which was right over the hill from her house on the outskirts of town), a place loaded with cattails, darning needles, dragon flies, pollywogs, two car radiators, a lot of green scum, and four or five old tires. Using a bow and steel-tipped arrows, she casually slaughtered the hapless frogs who lived on the edge of this mudhole, and she started a graveyard underneath the evergreen tree, using popsicle sticks for tombstones. There was no doubt but that she set a record for consuming Toasted Almond Good Humors simply to get at the sticks. The graveyard became pretty crowded ("I was quite a prolific little killer; must have had sixty or seventy funerals, and every one of those sticks had a name; I bet I got as far as Theophilus and

Thirza in the back of our dictionary ...''), then, sick of it all, she removed every weathered popsicle stick, smoothed over the ground, and read as a eulogy, a poem by Carl Sandburg, part of it going like so:

> Shovel them under and let me work.
> Two years, ten years, and passengers
> ask the conductor:

> What Place is this?
> Where are we now?

> I am the grass.
> Let me work.

Was it odd that a little girl of, say, eight or nine years, should be sitting cross-legged underneath an evergreen tree reading "Grass" to a lot of decomposed frogs' skeletons who didn't particularly give a damn? Not at all, because that's the way she was from the start. She got into books at the age of three or four and graduated to become an under-the-covers-with-a-flashlight addict, the reason she came up wearing glasses when only eleven. They were big owl's-eye glasses that, when she tilted them, caused the world to slide sideways, so much to her amusement that she wore the glasses constantly tilted, an affectation that in the long run developed her a pair of schizophrenic eyeballs doctors had never been able to figure out, nor she either. She often wondered what they could see in there, the doctors, their drops of light swooping around the inner sensitive curve, pinning down pictures that couldn't get through the rational strainer, trapped before they became thoughts, gaudy miniature convicts clinging obstinately to the concave walls, waiting to be shot, or maybe biding their time until they could break into the regulated turmoil of her mind. Well, what she actually thought about her eyes was "Bullguano, five times nine."

The important thing was she loved books, and whistled through the Jungle Book, Doctor Doolittle, Natty Bumpo and his crowd, the entire Oz series, and the Hardy Boys instead of Nancy Drew. Taste in books had inclined her toward hoydenism, exaggerated the tomboy she would have been anyway. All her life she had avidly followed Dick Tracy, Steve Canyon, Terry and the Pirates, Li'l Abner, and Rip Kirby in the daily comics, but had never once read Brenda Starr ("Yetch!") or Mary Worth ("Double Yetch!") or Winnie Winkle ("Yetchissimo!"). For building her vocabulary she had read all of Damon Runyon; for training her memory, she had learned "The Cremation of Sam McGee," "The Shooting of Dan McGrew," "The Ballad of Yukon Jake," and "The Lone Trail" by heart.

Outside of books, she had lived a consistently varied childhood, once winning twenty-seven cents for eating seven worms and a grub; again collecting every Topp's baseball card except Solly Hemus, then selling the entire collection to a "snot-nosed bastard" named Jay Farrell for a bag of penny jawbreakers. She would have had all the Straight Arrow cardboards for a year, too, had she not finally blown her lunch over her Shredded Wheat. She won a short story prize in the fourth grade for a three page graphic description of a small girl like herself who was shot to the moon in a rocket, where, upon landing, she was unfortunately decapitated by a meteor. And though perfectly normal brainwise, she felt she had had

[6]

a narrow escape from child psychiatrists, when, having gone into the bathroom one day, put the red shoebox on a chair, climbed up, dropped her drawers, bent over, and been in the midst of inspecting her rear end in the mirror, her mother had walked in, said "Oh, excuse me, please," and started to walk out, then turned disbelievingly and stammered; "What ... what in the name of Sam Hill are you *do*ing!" But the headshrinkers never materialized, and as for her rear end, she never bothered to look at it again: seen it once and you'd seen it for all time, unless you got fat or sprouted a boil, neither of which she'd done to date.

Then again, had her parents seen the way she handled kites, she might have spent her childhood in a strait jacket. All together, she must have manufactured a million kites out of newspapers, glue, and strips of cardboard or kindling, with old rags for tails. They weren't exactly what you'd call souped-up jobs, but occasionally they flew. The hitch was, whenever she got one good and up she cut the string and the kite sailed away out of sight, which somehow made her feel good—as if they were never going to come down. Wasn't there a kind of lonely ocean bird that spent all its life in the air? (She meant, of course, the Man-O'-War bird which spends the greater part of its sea-going life in the air.)

Among other things, she caused her parents fits by throwing a dozen eggs and half a jar of mayonnaise against the kitchen walls the night she had been one of the two elites in dancing class who sat out the "Boy's Choice." I could almost see tears well in her eyes while she described herself as a small gauzy heap of hope wearing smudged white gloves, a wilting taffeta dress, and oversized glasses, waiting with Cinderella smile to try on the glass slipper that never came. That same night she caught a jar of fireflies and tried to read by their light, but at the end of several paragraphs they died.

Recognition came to her at last when she volunteered to play "Silent Night" on the recorder for a school Christmas pageant, the only problem being she couldn't for the life of her play the recorder. She honestly tried to learn on the sly, but come the night of the big show, she flopped in monumental fashion. Sheer guts carried her on stage where she blew one high note for two minutes, plapping her fingers like mad up and down on the holes. Joe Grubner—with whom she was in love—told her to go to hell after the number when she tried to explain it to him backstage. He was a God-damned angel who got lowered from the ceiling on a wire. Pookie felt no better when the wire broke, dropping him four feet to the stage, for, being already a great athlete, he landed on his feet without a thump; made it look as if the wire had broken on purpose, in fact.

Jeered at by her classmates, ignored by Joe Grubner, she climbed into the Pemberton's apple tree where she stayed all night, or almost. She ate a billion green apples, got covered with dew, and fell out of the tree shortly after midnight. Her leg thoroughly broken, "Old Crab-Guts" Pemberton drove her to the hospital where she caught pneumonia and almost died, the only time except for tonsilitis at the age of three she was ever in a hospital.

Home again and healthy, she bought her first bra and a transparent white blouse through which Johnny Bianchi said he could see. She wore the blouse anyway for the next two weeks hand-running ... under a large brown lint-littered Shetland sweater.

In the fall of her freshman year in high school, she tried out for cheerleader, but the next day her mother sent a curt note to the principal telling him Pookie had a weak heart, and the principal informed Pookie that she had a weak heart, and she called him "Peachpit Pappas" right to his face, good for a week's suspension. Down but not out, she took up smoking and drinking and wearing falsies on account of being in love until the end of Time Immemorial with Joe Grubner, who finally took her to the Somerset Drive In on Route 5 to see Audie Murphy in "To Hell and Back." Right in the middle of the picture, he (Joe) reached inside her blouse, and though she afterwards cracked the joke—"Some of your bosom pals often turn out to be falsies"—he took back the ring he had given her an hour earlier, and they were no longer going steady. Posthumously, she deflated the old windbags every day, just a little bit at a time, hoping no one would notice, until she got down to the real thing, which admittedly wasn't much, and never would be for that matter, as I could plainly see, baggy sweater or no.

For quite a while after the Grubner fiasco she was very breast conscious. One evening while browsing through a romance magazine, she came across an advertisement which guaranteed her an "impeccable, fascinating, seductive bust" to be obtained through regular usage of a goo called The Bolivian Serum (a concentrated formula of llama milk that, upon application, was supposed to activate the secretion of the mammary glands, so that, within three weeks, a girl would boast a pair of knockers that even Superman would turn around for). She cut out the

[9]

coupon, circled one of six ("infantile, very small, deformed, pearshaped, saggy, overly opulent...") breast conditions, and included a money order for five dollars. Five dollars she might just as well have kissed away for all the good Bolivian Serum did her.

Time flew by, and, like everyone else, she suddenly found she had lost her childhood. It happened in the attic one wintry afternoon after school. The attic was dry; it smelled old and terribly interesting. Quiet memorable ghosts ruffled through the air, plucking their long-ago ballads on shriveled hearts; dropping their invisible footsteps on dry trunk tops; scraping their aery heads without hurt against a million sharp nail points. She could feel them moving to and fro; there was a comfortable sisss in the air. Rummaging around, she found a carton of old lead soldiers—most of them British who had tirelessly fought hours on end over old frogs' skeletons under the evergreen tree—and she set them up on trunks, hid them behind chair legs, crouched them beside a warped thirteen-dollar guitar, nestled them in a bouquet of paper flowers her father had given to her mother on one of their wedding anniversaries, placed them anywhere, in fact, that they seemed strategically to go. Then she sat on a trunk brooding over her work for two hours. There were no shots, nobody was even tipped over or dashed to pieces for the fun of it against the rough floorboards.

That same afternoon in the attic, she came across an old harp her mother had once tried to learn to play. The wooden part was scrolled with leaves and several cherubs' heads, the usual stuff, but what made it very ancient and sad was it had only one string intact. All the others had snapped, and now, like electric hairs, they jumped frozenly out from either side of the frame. Every now and then, when but a little girl lying awake at night in her bed, Pookie had thought she heard a sound, a muffled twung! in the darkness over her head, and it occurred to her suddenly this winter afternoon that the sounds she had heard long ago were the harp slowly dying, and with each string, the little hope that had been her mother's youth, and most likely her own also, going with it.

Some other time during that same winter or perhaps a later one, she took a hammer and pried the nails out of one of the tiny attic windows, and peeked outside where it had begun to snow. She imagined there was a big Pookie Adams up in the sky; the snowflakes were her tears. And she felt immensely sorry for herself because she would go through her entire life shedding beautiful crystalline tears that would melt against the warm earth: and she knew that day she would always be unhappy.

Her parents were (and always had been)—a. Wishy-washy; b. Turd-like; c. Inanities personified. Only once had either of them shown any signs of life in all the years she had known them. That was when her father had emptied the clip of a World War II souvenir pistol into the refrigerator, the direct result of an argument (the only one they ever had) over the way a breakfast egg had been cooked one Sunday morning when Pookie was not more than four or five. Although the day before it had rained like you never saw rain before, solid as if dumped out of a big wash pan, this Sunday bloomed bright and sunshiny, consequently she was rather surprised on coming downstairs late for her Cheerios to find her father (who was already rheumatic at thirty-five—or thought he was—and who hated rain and loved the sun) glowering at the

kitchen table, or, more specifically, at a plate of regal-
looking eggs (scrambled, creamy, and sprinkled with
parsley) sitting atop a thick Fanny Farmer Cook Book.
Pookie was even more surprised when, during the course
of breakfast, her father launched into a long tirade
against her mother, swearing among other things to pack
his bags and get out of there, go live in a hotel or boarding
house where he would have a little peace on earth without that bitch her mother nagging, nagging, nagging all
the time, and in fact, what he ought to do instead was tie
that woman to her bed and shove the Goddam eggs down
her throat!

Whereupon he stood up, the pistol in his hand, and
before you could raise your eyebrows and blink there
were five terrible explosions grouped together within a
second—POW! POW! POW! POW! POW—and the
whole place filled up quick with gunpowder smell. The
freezing unit motor let out a high whine, the fluorescent
light overhead flickered nervously, the white aluminum
door of the frig—now decorated with four gaping holes
(he had missed once)—swung open, and milk, orange
juice, and what had been a pitcher of lime Kool-Aid cas-
caded onto the floor. "That will teach your mother about
eggs!" he shouted, hurling the pistol into the dying frig
where it stabbed barrel-first into the side of the last un-
injured milk carton and quivered.

The point being that every Sunday morning Mr. Adams
(The Fat Balding Realty Broker) took Mrs. Adams (The
Fat Balding Realty Broker's Housewife) her breakfast
in bed, and every Sunday for years he had automatically
scrambled the eggs without ever having had a single complaint from his wife. On this particular morning, how-

ever, Mrs. Adams stuck up for her rights, complaining that she was never consulted as to her breakfast preference, and, instead of the usual scrambled eggs (of which she was mighty sick), she insisted on having nothing less than a boiled egg. That the complaint was lodged after the breakfast had been carefully (though automatically) prepared probably accounts for the reaction it was catalyst to. Pookie figured they had most certainly disliked each other all their married lives, but had such little stature as human beings that they supported each other through fear of the complications separation would incur: freedom to them was a kind of nuclear deterrent; the fear of it kept them together.

So, whenever she had a chance Pookie got away from home, and as good an excuse as any was Aunt Marian and Uncle Bob, who lived in Los Angeles, and from whose house she was returning. Uncle Bob's one claim to fame as her father's brother was that once while on a plane trying to fly from New York to Los Angeles in a thunder storm, he had found himself sitting next to—wonder of wonders—a movie star named William Brown. They set to talking about one thing and another, and somewhere in the conversation Uncle Bob managed to tactfully ask what movies William Brown had played in, and he learned that his green-looking seat partner had been (in his biggest role) the navigator of a Flying Fortress in a grade B World War II flick. Two or three times over the summer, Pookie had been at cocktail parties with Uncle Bob where he had slyly brought up the subject of famous personalities in order to get in his licks with "My good friend, Bill Brown." He usually became quite crestfallen when no one tumbled: "Who? William Brown? You mean

Willy? The Willy?'' Nevertheless, he sent William Brown a card every Christmas, and it would undoubtedly have warmed the cockles of William Brown's heart to witness the jubilation his annual New Year's card caused in Uncle Bob's household. Uncle Bob was a fifth grade school teacher, going on fifty; Aunt Marian did work with retarded children: they had no kids themselves. But they were good-natured, and a little pathetic, dying together in a matronly blowsy way. At any rate, Uncle Bob in Los Angeles was a damn sight better than her own folks in Merritt, and she certainly hated to return to school. Fie on it!

"Are you all done?" I asked.

"I don't know," she said thoughtfully; "can you think of anything I've left out?"

She had me there. I swear it didn't take her but five minutes to rattle off what I just gave you, and I wasn't about to set her off again.

So I said nothing; I chucked pebbles.

"How old are you?"

I told her: eighteen.

"Oh? You don't look that old. I'd take you for sixteen, or at the most, just a shade over seventeen; call it the near side of a whisper."

"The what?"

"The near side of a whisper ... just under the wire. I'm seventeen, I might add, senior this year—where do you go to college?"

"You the FBI or what?"

"That's me: actually I'm a tommy-gun in disguise." She frowned, lowered her head, puffed out her cheeks, and an amazing blib-a-dip tommy-gun sound came out of her mouth for a full twenty seconds until she choked for air.

In order to avoid any more of that, I explained I would be a freshman come fall, and I painted for her a picture of the New-England-white-chapel-on-top-of-a-hill-type college, eight hundred men, no women, that I had seen only once before when I went there for an interview.

She said, "I'd guess, from the way your sneakers are agitating the gravel, that you're probably curling your sweaty little toes under a mile a minute, wishing that loudspeaker would call us back into the relative safety of the bus. Most people I've met in my life have been reluctant to befriend me, but you're way out ahead in first place, I'm not kidding. I bet you were brought up on nails and tobasco sauce and little Jewish babies, weren't you?"

"Yeah." Very funny.

"Brother! You know, talking with you is like trying to catch butterflies on the wing with a pair of tweezers. Where have you been and what have you been doing all summer?"

I answered with a shrug, and scooped up some more gravel figuring if I ignored her she'd go away.

"You're getting the feel and the rhythm of it, aren't you? It's becoming more ordered, more aesthetically pleasing, if you know what I mean?"

"What is?"

"Your throwing. Close your eyes. Now, the regular plink-plink of gravel pellets could be like the dripping of a water faucet, see what I mean? Why don't you make a super-human effort and tell me where you've been?"

I told her I'd been in Red Brick, Arizona, working for a scientific laboratory.

"That's interesting; tell me what you did."

[15]

She had me there. I went into detail about the entire thing, because it had meant a lot to me: my two expeditions for the Government Forestry Service chopping down snags hit by lightening; hunting for snakes along the highway in the evening when they came onto the roads for warmth; riding horses down into green canyons on a deer count with the Fish and Game boys; shooting and later dissecting birds to see if they had filarial worms; helping to build a lizard colony, and later to take photographs and record their habits... I got hung up on Gloriosa beetles and old Dr. Culpepper who had danced a jig and given me a quarter for every live female beetle I brought him. I even took a match box out of my blue jean jacket pocket and showed her the beautiful gold-striped green bug inside. She ran her finger over it, feeling how the stripes were slightly raised, and suggested they might have been painted in enamel by a very fine brush. "What's it called again?" she asked, as I slid the box back into my pocket.

"A Gloriosa beetle."

"How do you find them?"

"Occasionally they bat against a lighted window. But more often, in the evening, while you're out walking under a tree or something, they drop to the ground in front of you. It's funny."

"Just out of nowhere..." She liked the idea.

"They gotta come from somewhere."

"They probably slide off wet leaves, all in fun, and then—zap! into the old ether. What a way to go." She snapped her fingers; "Like that."

I went on to tell her about catching Tiger beetles for Dr. Jacobbson, a noted entomologist, who put a male and female beetle together in a little glass jar, and then, smack dab in the middle of their copulation, dumped them out into a pan of boiling water, the only way to get an unharmed specimen of the male's penis for inspection.

"That's interesting," Pookie said; "I wonder if anyone has ever tried it with human beings. I'd be willing to donate Joe Grubner or Peachpit Pappas as guinea pigs. I'd even be willing to get them copulating if you'd only promise to spare me."

I certainly ignored that, going on as fast as possible about hunting for mite colonies in the desert, digging into the sand with a pocket knife, lifting the earth out almost grain by grain so as not to blunder into a colony and wreck it. Another big thing was grasshoppers; I had spent hours on the desert waving around a butterfly net, because mite larvae abounded behind grasshopper gills, and two scientists at the station were doing projects on mites.

"I once knew a girl who had a gill that grew out of her throat," Pookie said. "Her name was Sheila Carruthers."

"You what?"

"Can I help it if it grew out of her throat? They operated, and the operation left a little hole, and every now and then the hole would bleed so's she'd have to wear a scarf to school. The wildest purple and yellow scarf. People said her case was one in a million. I despised her; she had her picture on the front page of the *Gazette* and everything."

I asked her what in the hell she had said that for?

"Why ... I don't know. You were talking about gills and it occurred to me about Sheila ... Well, you *were* talking about gills, I presume?"

[17]

"I wasn't talking about gills, I was talking about mites, and I happened to mention, not throw it out as a general topic for discussion, that mite larvae could be found behind grasshopper gills."

"And so ...?"

"What?"

"So what's the difference between larvae and gills that makes one so acceptable to your conversation, and the other so unacceptable to your conversation, that's all I want to know?"

"Look; I can see you're not interested in scientific stuff ..."

"Not interested! How about the butterfly bush I planted next to the evergreen tree? How about the seventeen monarchs, six yellow tiger swallowtails, nine black swallowtails, four morning glories, two hummingbird moths, one luna moth, and ninety-seven billion cabbage butterflies I have in my collection at home, not to mention the dragonflies, rhinoceros beetles, katydids, June bugs, and the vinegaroon my Uncle Bob sent to me when he was vacationing in Tuscon? How about that—have you got a vinegaroon, Mr. High-and-Mighty?"

Not only did I have a vinegaroon (a very large whip scorpion that stinks like vinegar if you bug it), but I had to hit her with its Latin name, *Mastigoproctus giganteus,* to really fix her wagon, show her who she was fooling around with. Then I shut up. Why I didn't get up and walk away, I'll never know.

"Hey ... hey, come on now," she said quietly, leaning closer towards me. "I went too far, honest I did. I had no idea I was going to shout you into silence. If I'd known, I wouldn't have *dreamed ...*" She settled back and

[18]

shrugged. "I'm always doing that; I have a definite propensity for hanging myself. I feel miserable the minute I realize what I've done, but by then it's too late. If it helps any, I feel miserable. Rotten miserable."

I ventured an opinion: "Boy, are you ever nuts."

"Funny," she said. "A minute ago, remember? When I asked you what you did out there and your face lit up and you were happy all of a sudden, voluble too? Sooner or later I can get people to react that way if I poke around long enough looking for the soft spot, and every time it happens I think it's worth a million stars over Africa to have triggered that ... and then I blow it. Bang." She folded her hands in her lap and stared into the sky. "And you know what we're going to do now?" She wasn't talking to me, to anybody; just to air, to darkness. "We're going to sit here, side by side—bone silent. At first it will be a very awkward silence because we will both feel that having struck up a conversation before, we're indebted to continue it, but shortly the silence will become older, and grow vague, until eventually we'll stop fighting it, both at the same time, and peace will come to us. It'll be a comfortable peace, you may have known it at one time or another: sliding down into a full hot tub and just lying there, looking at tiny bubbles of air caught in the hairs on your skin—anything like that ..."

Then she went on to tell me what she was going to think about in the forthcoming silence. She was going to think of her Grandfather Adams who was a very tall skinny man with overpowering eyebrows and long white strands of hair like rutabaga roots growing down from his earlobes. He had been retired all the years she vaguely knew him (he died when she was nine), and she honestly had no idea of what he had done for work before.

Pookie loved her grandfather deeply, and she had her reasons. Once, while visiting him in Chicago, she became very excited over a comic strip called "Casey Ruggles" (a Western drawn by Warren Tufts), and she cut out the strip every day and pasted it into a scrapbook. When she returned home, she was very upset because the *Merritt Gazette,* being a weekly, didn't carry Casey. So she wrote her grandfather a long letter explaining her predicament. Thereafter, until the day he died, she received, at the end of each month, a fat long envelope full of Casey Ruggles strips.

But the thing she would concentrate on during the silence was one particular morning she had shared with him. It was his habit to get up every morning between five-thirty and six o'clock, patter down to the kitchen, and cook himself an egg, toast, and coffee. Pookie used to wake up with him—his big feet shuffling around in even bigger slippers always woke her—and they would eat breakfast together in the dark warming kitchen, Pookie in a pink quilt bathrobe covered with poodles, her grandfather in a sleep-and-wear blue suit that he had likely not sent to the cleaners since before the First World War, and this was the only moment of peace they had all day, because when her Grandmother Adams woke up the fur began to fly; she made a person hop until he or she was blue in the face. Doing things, doing things; she'd never learned how to let well enough alone.

Now: Pookie and her grandfather were in the kitchen one morning, water was bubbling on the stove, coffee and bacon smells were so thick as to be almost drug-like, when her grandfather spilled some egg yolk on his tie. He scraped it off with his finger, and (don't ask Pookie how), this led to a discussion of stomachs, in particular, cows' stomachs.

And this is what her grandfather told her: he said, "A cow has eleven stomachs."

If you've ever taken biology, you'll know he was making it up, probably for Pookie's benefit. But who was she to care? She had always remembered it, always would, and come what may, she would never cease feeling choked up almost to the point of tears when she thought of the two of them all alone in their calm pre-dawn breakfast world, discussing eleven-stomached cows, before her grandmother woke up and the fur started flying. If she had to choose, that would be one of her most memorable, most meaningful moments in life.

At this point the loudspeaker announced our bus, consequently we never got to sit in silence thinking about things. I returned to the seat I'd been in before and Pookie took up a new one—directly behind mine. We weren't, as she might say, "but a whisper" out of town, when she leaned over the back of my seat and did some kind of a dance on my shoulder with her fingers.

"Why don't you come back and sit with me?" she said. "We know each other now, so it's sort of silly for us to sit apart, don't you think?"

Right here I'd better take a minute to explain something. I, like Pookie, am an only child, and I have lived all my life in a comfortable little house in Riverdale. I respect my parents, however; respect them a great deal, love them, in fact, though they are very strict, my father (who is a banker) in particular. As a kid I was given both piano and guitar lessons, and the guitar took hold, so by the time I met Pookie I was a pretty good musician, although to be perfectly honest it was all mechanical, I don't think I could have improvised a note. Other than that, I was never very athletic, and had but few friends through high school—that is, prep school. In my studies I was inclined toward the sciences; I was (and still am) very much interested in nature, as you may have gathered earlier. My hobbies at various times were model trains, erector sets, chemical kits, collections of bugs, feathers, eggs, you name it, and some experimentation with electrical apparatus. I read very few comics because I didn't really enjoy them. Nothing much excited me, but I was seldom unhappily bored.

And the fact is, as far as girls were concerned, I was a prude. I'd been a loner (as differentiated from ''lonely'') through my younger days because that was the way I was happiest: my life was uncomplicated, and I wanted it to stay that way. Even four years at prep school hadn't changed me, and those monastic years certainly hadn't given me a great deal of first-hand knowledge on how to handle women, or even get along with them reasonably well. I wasn't a fairy-type kid, but I resented intrusion into my affairs, and the prep school girls I met at mixer dances I definitely felt I'd been suckered into were certainly my idea of an intrusion. Therefore, after the fall of my freshman year, I patronized no further dances. I repeat: I wasn't unhappy, I wasn't abnormal, I wasn't upset, I just considered it a lot of unnecessary trouble to rent a tuxedo, buy a corsage, and go through all the assorted rigamarole connected with dances, proms, women, etc. I figured girls would come along in later life when they were due to come along, and until then I would live as pleasantly as possible. When I met Pookie it hadn't yet occurred to me that "Later Life" might just possibly have already arrived, so I was idealistic, priggish, mistrusting, and surly with forward women, and you can imagine how Pookie seemed at first to me.

Okay; now that that's straight, I was where she had invited me back to her seat. Being fairly helpless under her attack, I acquiesced and slouched into an uncomfortable position beside her, though as far away as was possible in such a cramped space.

"I thought you were going to do a Charleston in the aisle, you looked so overjoyed," she said.

We gabbed. That is, she did. I grunted whenever I thought punctuation seemed appropriate. Somewhere along the way she grabbed hold of my hand and I damn near split a gut squirming down through the seat.

"Look," she explained; "I'm not some kind of Bluebeard trying to put you in my closet."

But I couldn't get anything through my head except that I somehow had to stall her off, so I tried to think of something to say real quick-like, and it came out; "What in hell do you think you're du-di-du-di-doing?" And I swear to God I had never stuttered before in my life!

Talk about furious! I suppose she had a right to be, but she overdid it a lot, asking me if my testicles hadn't dropped or *what* was the matter? Hearing a girl say "testicles" electrocuted me into numbness, and all I did was sit and listen with amazement while she lashed out at me.

"I'm going to tell you what it's all about," she said, "just in case, one, you never experience it all the born

[23]

days of your life, or two, you've already experienced it and thought you must have been out of your mind and decided after the first couple of times you wet your sheets and had a sadistic dream or woke up and caught yourself masturbating that you were some kind of a sex monster or something, and the only way to combat IT was to think yourself into sterility and stay away from broads, and if that's the case, Brother, here's hoping you can be saved!''

Her way of saving me was to explain how she had grappled with puberty and come out of it reasonably sane and at least capable of slinking into a drug store and asking for Kotex or Tampax or what have you without going through the entire color scale. She told me how she used to make up pornographic daydreams about herself and men, how she had been kissed, fondled, and raped time and time again by the likes of Clark Gable, Errol Flynn, Cary Grant...even Jimmy Stewart, who was by far the shyest of the lot and always got her out in an apple orchard or on the swinging couch suspended from the back porch ceiling of a ranch house in Wyoming, or New Mexico, or Colorado. Because she was too embarrassed to buy them, she filched ''Muscle'' magazines from newstands, and at night, safely locked in her room, she pored over pages and pages of Mr. Americas, although for a long time whatever was behind their bikinis remained nothing much more to her than ''a handy gadget to bring on a picnic'' from a joke she had once heard. There eventually came a time when she believed she was over-sexed, and she worried a lot over this: she'd heard stories, and she waited in terror for the day when she would become one of those girls on account of whom hot dogs were cut up in private schools. But it all proved to be a lot of poppycock, nothing strikingly unusual occurred, and, by listening around a bit, she came to the conclusion that she wasn't the Great Lone Pervert befouling a pristine world, and as soon as she figured that out, she never gave it another thought.

Of course, I wouldn't have admitted it to her, but she hit pretty close to home. My usually dormant imagination had taken me by surprise and gone on a gruesome rampage between the ages of thirteen and fifteen, and I had been more than a little ashamed and startled over what I was capable of thinking about. I had repressed the memory of those days as far back as possible, for although I heard a lot of rough talk at school, I never heard anyone admit to anything that sounded at all like what I'd been entangled with. I used to make up stories about myself and the female counterparts of Pookie's movie stars. I'd sneak into their Hollywood bedroom closets while they were out, then, when they returned home alone late at night and had gotten dressed in their gauzy shorty-type nighties, I'd burst out of hiding, rape them quickly, then afterwards—get this!—cut off their breasts and put them (the breasts) into a deep freezer I had in the cellar of my bachelor apartment. Another thing I did (and all this for the purpose of getting a stiff, mind you), I invented various sexual tortures such as rolling spiked wheels over the stomachs of nude girls tied to stakes in the ground, and that accomplished, taking pokers or broom handles ... You get the idea. And though I had sensed I was not as gruesome an oddball as I seemed, as I mentioned before, I never heard anyone else say that he had dreamed up comparable nausea. Then

[25]

to suddenly get it from a girl; and one I had known for about half to three quarters of an hour ...!

I'm not sure how it happened, she must have caught me off guard or something, but I suddenly found that we were kissing. She tried to get her tongue into my mouth and I almost fell over backwards trying to get away. I was adamant enough so that she soon gave up in disgust.

"What is it?" she asked. "Do I have something even my best friends won't tell me about? Talk about kissing corpses! You can stop trembling because I'm all through playing the part of the forward octopus for a while. You certainly are an assiduous backpeddler." She sized me up with her big eyes for a full minute, then said mechanically, as if quoting: "If you're lonely it helps to have someone you can love. You can't be happy anywhere all by yourself. No man is an island ..." Then, to confirm the tone of her voice; "Page sixty-five, *True Romance,* month of July."

I said, "I'm not lonely."

She snarled, "Lonely, schmlonely," folded her arms, slouched deep in her seat, and went to sleep.

I slid open the window a crack. A steady breeze came in and tousled her hair. Outside there was an early-morning light, barely perceptible, moving into the hills. I'll have to admit I began to soften toward her. About an hour had gone by when she said very distinctly, her eyes still closed but not at all asleep: "And Dr. Adams, we of the Nobel Committee take great pride in bestowing upon you, for your outstanding work with Glorious beetles, the Nobel Biology Prize of 19 ..."

"Gloriosa," I corrected sleepily; the rest of the trip

was a big nothing until I woke up reeking of dragon breath, and we were in St. Louis.

We breakfasted at a grubby table on coffee and English muffins. Both feeling played out after the night before, we talked very little. Finally the bus was announced; we stood up together, and Pookie stuck out her hand. I looked at it.

"I change here," she explained, her voice slightly bitter. "We're splitting up, Pal."

"Oh. How do you go home?"

"I go to Terre Haute. There a small bi-plane takes me over five hundred miles of teeming swampland and two hundred miles of frozen tundra to my cozy little home in Merritt where Mommy and Daddy, God bless their Nothingness, greet me at the hangar and whisk me off to a Ho-Jo's for a shake and fries; it's been real—cheers."

I found my seat on the bus and talked with her a few minutes more through the open window before the departure. She seemed very sad, and with a half-baked chuckle, said; "I bet what my face resembles you could lay over the edge of a table like a Dali watch, couldn't you?" an allusion which completely escaped me at the time.

With that, the bus started up, and as it was backing around to head out, she suddenly exclaimed, "Hey! Wait a minute! What in hell's your name? I mean, I don't even know your name, for Christ's sake! I've been talking so much I forgot to ask you! Lord, when I die they'll have to sew my lips shut to keep me quiet!"

So I told her.

"Jerry who?"

And I gave her my last name, Payne, but she wasn't satisfied with that either, and asked for my address. I shouted it to her as we turned the corner, then she was out of sight.

I was still looking back when she ran around the corner into view, skidded to a stop, and, unbalanced, one foot swinging wildly in search of solid ground, waved goodbye.

CHAPTER TWO

SHE must have written down my address right away after I left, because I received seventeen letters from her between September and Valentine's Day, all of them forwarded up to school from Riverdale. My father wrote me three or four times asking what was he running down there, a forwarding service? and would I please write the young lady, informing her of my college address? I didn't for a long time, though, and when I got around to it at last, I blew it: royally.

Her letters were the work of a definite nut. She described how her senior year in high school was going, and how it wasn't going too. Mostly wasn't, I might add. She enlarged upon events without fear, one of the benefits from having a correspondent as removed as I was. In fact, she outright lied time and time again. A few examples:

Her high school football team went undefeated and copped the Indiana State Championship. (I later found out from her they had lost all their games.)

The East wing of the school was burned almost to the ground by an arsonist from City Hall during the November Caucus when school taxes were a big issue. (The facts behind this were that a janitor had accidently tossed a lighted match into the wastepaper basket in his own broom closet, and had put out the fire unaided five minutes later.)

Perennial enemy Sheila Carruthers had her leg amputated after falling off her uncle's tractor onto the sickle-bar. (As it turned out, this story developed from a trip Sheila had taken to the doctor's to have some plannert warts burned off.)

Joe Grubner climbed to the top of the school flagpole on a bet, got blown off balance, and, had he not caught his foot in the rope, would have fallen to his death long before the volunteer fire department arrived with its hook and ladder. (True, Joe climbed the flagpole: he went up in five minutes, came down in fifteen seconds, collected his money, and walked jauntily away.)

And so on, page after page.

On the up and up, she recounted to me many things that happened to her the exact way they happened. There was an evening in early December when, with her old white figure skates and a shovel, she went over to the Tadpole Pond, spent an hour clearing the ice, skated for fifteen minutes until her arches collapsed, then lay down on the bank and let herself be covered with snow that was falling. You could see the stars, but snow was falling. She quoted "Stopping by Woods on a Snowy Evening" in the same letter. Hardly a letter arrived, in fact, that didn't have several quoted lines in it illustrating some adventure or emotion.

It must sound strange when I say I never wrote her, not even once during all that time, but I don't know. I got used to her letters coming in, and she never once complained of my lack of correspondence, so I took her letters for granted, I rationalized that since we did not, in any sense of the word, know each other, I had no obligation to reply. I will say one thing, though; I never showed those letters to anyone else for the purpose of laughing over what a nut she was. So perhaps even then without my really knowing it, her oddness had touched me.

Her Christmas card was a real gem. Not really a card, but rather a vignette written in very neat script on a fancy kind of almost-parchment paper, it was entitled:

A PARABLE OR SOMETHING

and went like this:

Once upon a time there was a girl in love with a boy who didn't even know she existed, but that didn't throw her, for she knew that one day he would realize that she was his Eternal Love. This girl had one particular dream about the boy that she freuded up into her mind every night. It happened on a spring evening with her in her room throwing darts at her geometry book. The window was half way open; a breeze full of apple blossoms and lilacs was blowing into the room. Far away she could hear the shouts of kids playing one-a-cat in a neighborhood lot. She imagined lazily how they probably couldn't see the ball anymore, but she knew kids loved to challenge darkness; loved to try and bat a big soft white ball as if it were a tricky soap bubble that needed to be exploded —though she didn't know why. Anyway, suddenly she heard a voice calling her name softly, and she stopped throwing darts and went to the window.

It was the very boy she loved standing there, moonlight rippling through his tousled hair turning it to silver,

[31]

big eyes full as plums turned upward, a guitar ready in his hands to serenade her.

"Darling...?" he said, his voice trembling.

"Yes?" the girl replied.

"Oh, my Darling Darling Girl," he uttered, his voice pregnant with emotion; "I can't live another minute without you!" and he struck a passionate chord on his guitar.

"Of course," replied the girl, letting her eyes half close dreamily, allowing a Mona Lisa smile to flush her lips and daintily rouge her cheeks; "but why aren't you in college?"

"Darling; Light of my Life; Love of my Heart and Life of my Soul—I quit. I've been hitch-hiking for three days and three nights across the wide cruel country, just to come to you. Oh Blessed Angel, I want to marry you right now, will you have me? I don't have any money or anything, but we'll make ends meet somehow. We'll go South, drifting along the sleepy roads in dreams, we'll make love in the sweet fluorescent light of night-blooming cotton fields, we'll sing songs in the early misty mornings to awaken the birds, living our life on love alone..."

"Oh, Darling..." the girl said, and she straightaway climbed out her window, hung from the ledge for a moment, then dropped into her mother's petunia bed. He was all over her before she could utter a sound, covering her with kisses, tearing off her clothes. In two minutes flat they were making love on the close-cropped spring grass, the real way, naked as Adam and Eve. Then, thoroughly pooped, they lay still, breathing deeply; the grass prickled comfortably against the girl's back. The boy snuggled his head against her neck while his hands like summer streams gently massaged her body, and a blanket

[32]

of moonlight flapped out of the sky like a gauzy hand-kerchief dropped by a beautiful woman. The girl watched it come and settle on top of them. A chorus of green luna moths fluttered in the air above them, wings tincellating sonorously, humming Elizabethan love ballads...

Which is usually where the girl woke up, clutching a pillow to her breast, sweating to beat the band. She had a teddy bear with a ring in its head: if she pulled on the ring it played a song—that's the way she comforted herself.

Then one day the boy really did come, and you know what happened?

"Darling...?" he called, his voice trembling.

"Yes?" the girl replied.

"Darling, I've come to marry you and take you off to palaces where white horses roam through gardens of glass flowers, and fountains are rainbows that send liquid color in rivulets over the earth, and stars tick against the window panes at night."

"How delightfully exquisite," mooned the girl, and blew him a tender kiss from the tips of her lily-white fingers.

Then she climbed out the window and fell off the ledge. She landed on the boy's head, smashing to bits the beautiful guitar with which he had been planning to serenade her, so instead of making love, they spent hours crawling around in the grass collecting little pieces of lacquered wood that had been the guitar.

(At this point there was a crudely crayoned picture of a reindeer, and beneath the picture, in enormous bright letters:)

HAVE A COOL YULE
QUENCH YOUR THIRST ON THE FIRST
Pookie

I wrote to her at last in February. My letter would not have won any prizes for warmth. In fact, after the volumes heaped upon volumes she had sent me, mine must have been an out-and-out insult. It followed the usual asinine line: Dear Pookie, I'm sorry I haven't written sooner but you know how college is, lots of things to do and not much time to do them in. We had rushing the first few weeks, and we've been having Hell Week lately, and I bought a new electric guitar, a Gretsh, and a real beaut. My classes aren't so bad, I have three on Monday, Wednesday, and Friday, and ... It has been snowing here all day and now we have about two feet of the doggone stuff, and I wish it were spring. That about wraps it up because nothing much of interest has happened so far, and I really can't think of anything more to say, and besides it's time to hit the hay. Drop me a line when you get a chance, I appreciate your letters. Take care and be good—Sincerely, Jerry.

She sent me one last letter, obviously written with great care, from the hospital where she was recuperating from an accident she later rather casually referred to as the Valentine's Day massacre, in which she shared front page headlines in most of the Indiana newspapers along with friends of hers: Joe Grubner, Jay Farrel, Johnny Bianchi, Karen Boise, and Sheila Carruthers. It was a bad accident; a long letter...

... The night started out fine, the way most nights are supposed to when there is an accident. Joe drove us to his father's summer cabin after the Heart-to-Heart sox hop in the gym. Perched on some mossy rocks, half hidden by pines, overlooking a frozen lake, it is a perfect log cabin, complete with deerheads, a bearskin rug, Coleman lanterns, and greasy decks of cards, everything smelling of pine pitch. We built a fire in the huge fireplace, then sat around drinking bootleg beer and whiskey, compliments of Joe himself, Valley High's greatest athlete. Later, Joe and I went for a walk. It was very cold but clear, snow on the ground and snow coating a thin layer of ice on the lake, but none in the air. It was about the first time I thought I was maybe going to like Joe a little, and vice-versa.

Before we could decide, however, we returned to the cabin, thence home. We didn't get very far: Joe tried to take a right-angled curve leading onto a small frame bridge at sixty miles an hour, and needless to say, he failed to make it. We turned over about thirty times on our way down to the creek, then we stopped, upside down, the tires not even whirring because the car was like a ball of paper that had been crumpled in a giant fist.

Naturally, I thought I was dead, but on the contrary, I was simply lying in a patch of snow and old leaves, comfortable as you please, except when I tried to move, I couldn't. Johnny Bianchi was a few feet away, pinned beneath the car, his head and one arm showing. He was trying to say something: I could see the words bursting out of his mouth, even feel them, but I couldn't hear a thing. Joe was halfway into the creek trying to crawl out, except he couldn't because he had been shattered, all but his head and a little of his heart, I think: his whole body was like the broken leg of a dog; he was trying to drag it with his powerful arms, all the time gasping, "Now I've done it, now I've God damn done it, but good have I done it!" He was crying, either from shock, or because Johnny Bianchi was his best friend. He was too beat up to be crying from physical pain. The other kids—Jay, Karen, and Sheila—were still inside the car: they had to be dead.

The first thing I said was, "Joe, will you kindly shut up?"

He stopped everything: crawling, gasping, crying. He made a choked bloop sound and a glob of red snot came out his nose. I remembered that he had always been a beautiful athlete, the kind you would want to inscribe on a commemorative stamp: crew-cut blond hair, strong dumb friendly face, perfectly proportioned physique, comfortably complacent brain—you could really only think of him posing for a picture, veins of sweat running through charcoal blotches under his eyes, and behind him a crazy bright crowd attacking the goalposts.

He stared at me and I at him. His eyes described the whole trajectory of a bad day, from insanity through hatred to drowsiness. There followed between us a quaint wooden conversation. I began it:

"Is the water cold?"

"I don't know, I can't feel it."

"Do you think someone will come soon?"

"Maybe. I don't know."

I remembered an important thing I'd always meant to ask him—how much money he'd won the day he climbed the flagpole.

"Five dollars."

"Were you scared?"

"No; not very much."

"Not even at the top?"

"Least of all at the top."

"Did you feel like a king?" If I kept him talking I felt I might keep him alive.

"No."

"What then?"

"Like myself."

"Did you want to come down?"

"Sure. Why not?"

"I would have stayed as long as I could." I would have, too.

He tried to laugh, bitterly I suppose, but only succeeded in ejecting another red gob out his nose. He closed his eyes.

"Are you asleep, Joe?"

"Yes."

"I don't think you should go to sleep."

He didn't answer.

"I'm going to tell you a Little Audrey joke, then." And without waiting for his go-ahead, I began. It was the one where she's in a boat with her boyfriend. They have three cigarettes and a pack of matches between them, but the matches are wet, they won't strike. Little Audrey asks for one of the cigarettes, which he gives to her, and she promptly throws it overboard. He gets mad, wants to know why she did that, but Little Audrey just laughs and laughs and laughs.

"You want to know why?" I must have asked him two or three times over, but he never answered, so I answered it myself: "Because she knew that made the boat one cigarette lighter," and hearing my own voice talking to just myself really scared me for a second.

[37]

Well, Pookie Adams, you are crazy, I thought. All night long you have been play-acting, dancing around on your tippy toes, shooting off a blank pistol, and one by one your protagonists have fallen onto the stage, and now you are behind the curtain and something is wrong, nobody is rising to take the encores: you and five dummies, a platinum brook, cardboard trees, and a lot of styrofoam snow...

Here's what finally happened. For a long time no one came to our rescue. After about an hour, Johnny Bianchi —who had been silent all this time—suddenly vomited blood. His head jerked back and forth, and his hand flapped uselessly against the side of the car. Then his head stopped shaking, but his hand continued flapping, though intermittently, and that was the only sound—the occasional tap-tap of his hand until he died, and I was alone. No wind blew because it was early morning. The brook made little inane bubbling sounds. Again and again I tried to move but I seemed to be paralyzed. In my mind I began to hum a tune that you've probably heard on the radio; it's getting to be very popular:

Transfusion, transfusion,
Oh, Doc, I got the cotton-pickin' convalusions;
I'm never never never gonna speed again—
Slip the blood to me bud! *

Once I'd begun it was impossible to stop. Like when you're in bed at night and you suddenly become aware of the glands in your mouth secreting saliva. You're cooked; you have to swallow every ten seconds.

Mr. Lawrence Anderson and his nephew Wayne dis-

* From "Transfusion," recorded by Nervous Norvus on the Dot label, © Paul Barrett Music, Inc.; used by permission.

covered us. They fell from nowhere, a couple of nervous mittened parachutists in enemy territory. The nephew took one peek inside the car and promptly upchucked on the front tire. Mr. Anderson lugged Joe out of the water and puttered over his body, tweaking his overcoat buttons, wondering what to do. During the several minutes they failed to notice me, I felt like an electric eye watching a couple of inept bank robbers at work. When they startled upon me at last, Mr. Anderson could think of nothing to do but give me his mittens, at the same time admonishing me to have courage until he got the police. The nephew suggested they carry me up to their car for warmth, but Mr. Anderson said certainly not, because if I died, they might be held responsible, and my parents could sue them for their every last penny. Then they scrambled up the bank to safety, the last time I saw them, and I must say I was relieved.

By the time an ambulance came I had grown used to being frozen solid and picking tiny snow goobers off Mr. Anderson's mittens and gazing at the car and Johnny and Joe. I was mad, in fact, when the army of accident technicians moved in on the scene.

Well, like in the "Ancient Mariner," I alone have lived to tell the tale: Joe died from internal hemorrhages three hours after they got him to a hospital. I'm in the hospital myself, having sustained some sort of sprained vertebra, but nothing serious—the paralyzation was only temporary, due mostly to shock. Being in here is not too bad, since . . .

(At this point she must have received my lovely effort, for she broke off writing abruptly, and when she resumed several days later, it was in a different vein from her description of the accident.)

...Jerry Payne, of all the cross-eyed square-toed pink-phalanged five-uddered knuckle-brained clapp-congested audastic atavistic Bavarian Yeti sons of cabbage-headed hogbody bigluvulating bastards, YOU TAKE THE ROYAL CAKE!

How devastatingly wonderful it was to receive your letter the other day; however did you find the time to write such an informative and captivating piece of shit? So you say it's snowing out your way? Then be sure to wear your golf shoes when you go walking, won't you? Otherwise you might slip and break your stinking neck, and they would have to stuff you in your Grutch guitar case and drop you in a big hole in the ground, and we wouldn't want that, not much we wouldn't, would we? I guess I'll call it quits now: time to hit the hay, though it's only nine o'clock. Up bright and early in the morning for temperature readings and intravenous feedings, you know.

Don't hurry about dropping me a line in the near future as I still haven't found the time to read all your previous scintillating letters. You certainly are a loquacious fellow!

Pleasant dreams! Remember me to your mom and your Uncle Bill who comes on weekends.

Very deeply sincerely yours,

Pookie!

PS. If I had a Glorious beetle, I'd feed it cyanide for a week, then I'd bake it in a cake and send it to you. But I don't, so I won't.

PPS. If someone were to suddenly send me a couple of
asps, I'd crawl into a tower and commit suicide.
PPPS. *Merde!* That's French for the bum you are.

(And I heard no more from her, nor she from me.)

When I wrote to Pookie that little of note had occurred
during my freshman year, nothing could have been further from the truth. You see, that was the year I woke up.
To begin with, I made up my mind to join a fraternity,
because ninety per cent of the college did. I figured things
would be most comfortable that way, and no one would
intrude upon my life more than was at minimum neces-
sary.

I figured wrong; real wrong.

The hell-bent-for-election chaos of rushing took place
the first week, and with it my troubles, mountains of them,
began. They were compounded by my two roommates,
fellows by the names of Roe Billins and Harry Schoonover, who impressed me right off the bat as being out-
and-out animalistic clods. Harry Schoonover, who went
by the name of Schoons, was a short, blocky, almost bald,
blue-eyed, half-toothless, banana-nosed boy, who (I was
quickly able to gather) idolized drinking, fornicating, and
hockey in that order. I didn't have to wait very long to
learn about the drinking part; it manifested itself not
more than an hour after I had unpacked my suitcase on
that first lonely day.

I was lying on my bed in the dormitory section of our
two-room suite, idly seducing the elephant-uddered *Play-
boy* centerfolds that Schoons had somehow managed, during his few short hours at school, to tape all over the

ceiling, when, puffing like steam engines, Roe and Schoons banged into the living room lugging a case of cold bottled beer which they forthwith began to consume.

"Have one!" Roe shouted in to me. "It's on the house." He was a very tall (6' 4") anemic guy, with sandy hair, little squinty eyes, and enormous ham hands that made anything from a pencil to a beer can look like a miniature. There was a sarcastic twang to his voice that I didn't like at all. But then, his manner of speaking was nothing compared to Schoons, who chattered fifty per cent of the time in some alien tongue that, as I got to understand it better, turned out to be nothing more than a collegiate brand of slang.

I said no thanks to the beer and went back to staring at the ceiling while they drank and gabbed and very shortly became drunk.

At which point, Schoons charged into the bedroom and from under his bed produced a hockey stick, from his suitcase a puck. Back in the living room, he removed the asbestos sheet from in front of the fireplace and lined up four or five empty bottles across the hearth.

"Let's hand out a few fatties to those weightless lagers!" he hooted. Fatties—as far as I could ever make out—have something to do with pain.

The first puck he let fly from the opposite end of the room not only neatly pulverized one bottle, spraying glass all over the room, but it damn near went through the fireplace it was shot so hard. The ricochet hit the door jamb to the bedroom and came within an inch of shearing off my nose. Schoons thundered into the room, retrieved his puck, gave me a half grin, half snarl which I imagine was supposed to convey that he was having fun, then went back to work with amazing efficiency.

The truth of the matter is, Schoons was an excellent hockey player who later on in the year was to become, though only a freshman, one of the better defensemen on the college varsity team. He was also to acquire a bit of infamy when, thirty seconds after skating out to his defense position in the opening game of the season, a puck cleaned the teeth from his upper jaw. Coach Kelly later sniffed the puck and suspected it smelled of alcohol, which, no doubt, it did: Schoons considered it good luck to have been drunk at the time, otherwise the pain would have been unbearable.

Back in the room, an hour or so later when we were besieged by the first wave of upperclassmen seeking to amuse us, the last of the lagers had been dealt their fatties: chairs were overturned, puddles of beer were spreading into corners, and a blanket of broken glass covered the floor. The upperclassmen were vastly impressed that a couple of frosh could make themselves so much at home in so short a time with such apparent ease, and off we went to begin a week of booze, prolonged handshakes, friendly pats on the back, guided tours of houses, big and little intrigues, and ultimate incredible emotional confusion.

Right from the start I made no bones concerning how I felt about the boozing, get-drunk attitude of those who purported to entertain me. I carried my white banner of purity among the pigs, and, though they constantly grunted me down, I rose from each encounter flag in hand, more aloof than ever before. Consequently, after the first night, my invitations dwindled, until, near the close of the week, I for the most part had my nights to myself. It was obvious by then that I would not be useful in swaying Roe and Schoons to one house or another, and my other quality—that of being able to play competent highbrow guitar—was worth very little. In short, though at the start of rushing I may have looked on paper like an important member of the triumverate, I looked it no more: it had taken the public at large about three days to brand me a "turkey."

Well; I thought I didn't care, but I had a hard time convincing myself. I went to bed early those last several nights and for hours listened to the sounds around campus; cars starting and stopping, doors slamming, boys cursing good-naturedly, boys laughing, irregular footsteps clopping down the hall, muffled giggles—all sounds of fun. But I had committed myself, and I clung to my condemnation of the orgy, although I must have subconsciously kicked myself a hundred times a day for doing so. Thinking back, it is quite surprising how friendly Roe and Schoons were to me all during this period, considering the cold shoulder I gave to them. But maybe they were more farsighted than I; maybe they could see my potential.

I awoke the final day fully expecting to land in the Pig Pool, the group of boys who have received no bids and who are split up among the fraternities that failed to make their quotas. But luck was with me, I received one bid, surprisingly from the fraternity—and it was a good one—to which Roe and Schoons had been pocket-pledged for several days. Having seen in subsequent years how the system works, I can now envision Roe and Schoons standing up before the brothers in some secret meeting that took place during that week, arguing in my behalf, saying I was not such a bad guy, just a little mixed up, that's all, I could really pick an ax, I would be good for the house academic average, and therefore I would be an excellent candidate to fill out the quota. "You guys'll see," I can hear Schoons saying; "Payne'll come around; it's only a question of time."

Whatever the case may have been, I got my one bid, and I accepted. It was not, however, a triumphant moment for me when one of the upperclass brothers to whom I had not previously spoken a word fixed a pledge pin to my sweater and vigorously shook my hand: I felt humiliated; I damn near cried.

Then there was my coming around: as Schoons might have said, it was a question of time; a long, painful time. Of the fourteen boys in our pledge class, I soon learned that I was bottom guy on the totem pole; The Scapegoat. I made matters no easier for myself with my frosty attitude toward the business of being a pledge. Rather than submit good-naturedly to the hazing, I defied it, refusing to do the menial tasks assigned to me, refusing to learn my pledge lessons, refusing to light cigarettes when ordered to do so—and so on, through a hundred little kowtows.

My unpopularity soon reached a crescendo. Then— much to the dismay of Roe and Schoons who, when not singing praises to Bacchus' name, were worshipping at Morpheus's temple—there came many nights when I was ripped loudly from my bed at two or three in the morning and run across campus to the fraternity house, where, in the dankness of the basement television room, I was put under the lamp, a lone one-hundred-watt bulb that shone in my eyes while the brothers gave me the third degree. This was a strenuous and somewhat terrifying affair.

"What's your name, Pledge?" the prosecutor would begin.

"Jerry Payne."

"Jerry Payne, what, Pledge?"

"Jerry Payne, Sir."

"You lie! What's your name, Pledge?"

"Jerry Payne, Sir."

"You lie again, Pledge! Do you know what your real me is?"

"No."

"No, what, Pledge?"

"No, Sir."

"That's better. Now, you know what your name is, Pledge?"

"No, Sir."

"What *are* you, Pledge—an imbecile?"

"No, Sir."

"What?"

"I mean, Yes, Sir."

"Yes, Sir, what, Pledge?"

"Yes, Sir, I'm an imbecile, Sir."

"You're damn right you're an imbecile, Pledge!"

"Yes, Sir."

"Now, you know what your name is, Pledge?"

"No, Sir."

"It's whaleshit, Pledge!"

"Yes, Sir."

"Alright: what's your name, Pledge?"

"Whaleshit."

"Whaleshit, *what,* Pledge!"

[46]

"Whaleshit, Sir!"

"YOU LIE, PLEDGE! WHAT'S YOUR NAME!"

This line of question-and-answer went on sometimes for as long as two hours, or at least until they tired of the game or I seemed dangerously close to a breakdown. How many were the times I stumbled away from that house drenched in sweat, and made my way back to the freshman dorm almost as a blind man, with the shocking white image of the lamp bobbing ahead of me; how many were the early morning hours I lay exhausted in my bed, plotting the mass execution of the brothers!

But perhaps the most ingenious, most hateful torture they contrived for me, was making me the Keeper of the Hound.

The hound's name was Poopsick. He was a mongrel puppy someone had picked up in a bar, a very cute little dog, all black but for a white diamond on his chest, and all the brothers loved him dearly. All the brothers except me, that is: I detested Poopsick with all my heart, and then some!

Because, you see, Poopsick, who was not the least bit housebroken, had diarrhea, the worst case of diarrhea any dog anywhere on this earth has probably ever had. Being Keeper of the Hound meant that I was called to the phone in my wing of the freshman dorm at least six times a day and ordered over to the house on the double to clean up Poopsick's latest mess. If I refused, the phone rang every fifteen minutes for several hours, and then, in the afternoon or evening, depending, if I still hadn't responded, a delegation of the stronger brothers collected me from wherever I was—the gym, the biology lab, the library, it made no difference—and carried me bodily over to the house and set me down before my task. One day, when in the morning I had emphatically declared I would never again scrape two shirt cardboards together to pinch up another Poopsick pie, I returned to my room after classes and found a neat little heap of excrement sitting on my pillow. From then on I went when I was called, and believe me, that was often.

I fumed. I fumed and decided a thousand times to quit, then vowed another thousand times to stick it out. I had the feeling that they wanted to drive me out, and I was damned if I'd let them do that. Whether they liked it or not, I was there to stay: but what a miserable way of staying!

"You can't lick 'em, join 'em," Schoons admonished.

"You certainly aren't making it very tough or anything for yourself," Roe said.

"Bend like a willow in the breeze," Schoons advised.

"I hate those mothers, every one of them!" was my reply.

"Well; I sure am glad you're not getting kicked around much," Roe said, and off they went to do their laundry and while away the afternoon in the Village Tavern.

I fumed until Hell Week arrived in mid-January. If I had thought things were bad before, they were nothing compared to what was in store. To begin with, all the pledges' heads were shaved and we had to wear woolen clothes, but with no underwear. I decided the hell with it, I would wear what I pleased, and the next thing I knew I was running around the house in a foot of snow lugging a mattress on my back and shouting at the top of my lungs: "I dreamt I carried a mattress in my Maidenform undies!" They ran me until I dropped, then carted me inside and made me sit in the center of the living room on top of a large cake of ice in a washtub. Naturally, I had to do this with nothing between my sensitive pink fanny and the ice, and a day or so later I developed a case of piles, or anyway . . . a gigantic itch, that all the K-Y Jelly in the world couldn't cure.

I won't go through the entire week: suffice to say it was miserable. At the close of the first day I was so tired I couldn't have cared less what I went through, and from then on I was docile as a baby: I acquiesced readily to being the human bowling ball that had to roll down the length of the living room and knock down the human ten pins; I sat willingly in the basement phonebooth for hours on end happily screaming passages from the Bible until I lost my voice; I allowed them to dress me up in ten overcoats and call me Nanook from the North as sweat mixed with my wooly clothes and made me think I would die of itching; I stood for long hours in the plebe stretch, hands out in front of me, listening dumbly to the obscenities the brothers heaped upon me; and I ate the porridge with onions and salt in it that had a raw egg tinted with blue vegetable coloring on top, blew my lunch, and ate some more . . . Thus, my rebellious spirit broken, I trudged from humiliation to humiliation with nary a peep. Of course, I was not alone in all this: in fact, there were times when I almost liked my fellow pledges, seeing them also suffering in such stoical silence. For once, at last, I forgot to be indignant.

After several centuries of fun and games, the night of the Scavenger Hunt—by tradition the last event— arrived. We weary pledges assembled in the living room and were read a list of things that we had to bring back by midnight: autographed panties, buckets of cowpies, the moosehead from a bar, a live chicken, and so on. I was commissioned to fill a mayonnaise jar with no less than five hundred living specimens of *blatta orientalis*, that is, cockroaches. I took my jar in my mittened hands, and, along with Roe and Schoons, stepped outside into a blizzard.

"Somebody must be kidding," Roe moaned. He and Schoons had been charged with the cowpies.

"I'd like to give those bastards a few fatties," Schoons said, and he laughed half-heartedly.

"Cowpies," Roe whined. "Where on a night like this are we gonna find cowpies? One thing; I'm sure glad it's not snowing."

We all three burst out laughing and headed across campus in the snow. It was literally impossible to see three feet in front of us, and wind was driving the snow so that after half a minute of walking against it we were white from head to toe.

"What are you guys gonna do?" I asked.

"Get a bucket and a shovel and hunt us up some goodies," Schoons replied.

"Boy, am I glad it's not snowing," Roe said; "Because otherwise it might be cold out."

"Are you gonna find a barn or what?" I asked.

"That's right, Boomaga." Schoons had recently taken to calling me that—why, I don't know. "We're gonna find ourselves a twitty bird barn, yes indeedy."

"Why don't you join the show?" Roe suggested. "There probably aren't many cockroaches hanging around barns, them being so clean and all."

Barns, we agreed, were to be found on the other side

of town; pails and shovels were not to be worried about until we found a barn; if we ever found one.

Now, in all probability, we not only would have found a barn, but also a pail, a shovel, and sufficient cow patties for the occasion, plus my quota of cockroaches. As luck would have it, however, our path through town led past the Village Tavern. We walked by on the opposite sidewalk, our shoulders hunched, our hands shoved down into our respective boilers, our hair stiff and white, even our eyelashes frozen. Roe had just finished saying he was sure glad it was winter because that was the only time of year you had the opportunity to damn well freeze yourself to death, when Schoons, who was slightly in the lead, held up his hand and said, "Hold!"

"Hold, what?"

"Hold, what do I spy yonder?"

"Prithee; that's a rare sight," Roe said, following Schoons' finger which pointed across the street where we could just make out the illuminated three-ring Ballantine sign.

"Methinks we've stumbled across an ale house!" Schoons shouted into the wind.

"P'r'aps there be an ale or two inside," Roe said.

"Fellow tinkers, what think ye?" Schoons demanded.

"It's a fearful night for 'untin' manure," Roe said.

"Then—run f' y' tankards, laddies!" Schoons yelled, and he was the first one across the street and into the warm interior of the tavern.

What happened next isn't very clear in my mind. I met Ronnie, the grizzly but very friendly bartender who was delighted to see that Roe and Schoons had allowed neither the weather nor Hell Week to keep them from their customary Friday evening appearance at his establishment. Actually, I met Ronnie quite a number of times, for Schoons seemed to get quite a kick out of introducing us, especially as the evening wore on. Each time we met, Ronnie smiled his tobacco-y smile and shook my hand, and shouted, "I'm glad t' meet ya, God dammit all anyway, whattaya say?" A lot of toasting and shoulder slapping went on, then there arrived a time when Ronnie and Roe and Schoons were all looking down at me with startled expressions on their faces, but pretty soon their hands reached for me, and their faces, laughing now, were around me once again in their accustomed places. I fell in love with them, and we hugged one another, even Ronnie got into the act, and then there were a lot of dimes on the wet bar top glistening like stars, and Schoons was fighting with his blunt fingers to pick one up which he finally succeeded in doing, and the next thing I knew the juke box was playing "Stardust," and sure enough, we began to float and it was like being in a cloud, or on a cloud, or actually being a cloud, and the dimes kept disappearing from the counter. "Stardust" came on again and again, then there were some more dimes, stretching almost from one end of the bar to the other, and there were a lot of glasses, too—empty glasses with foam draining down their insides, and, inevitably, there was a crash, but Ronnie only laughed and shook his head and declared we were the craziest, God dammit all anyway, whattaya say. Then I suddenly found myself being propelled, without a coat on or anything, out the door, and a few minutes passed with me hanging over a snowbank, supported by Schoons and Roe, throwing up I suppose. Then I went to sleep: I dreamed of "Stardust" and my friend, Ronnie, and, very vaguely, of cockroaches, and being under a lamp.

When I woke up (miraculously back in my own bed) wishing I were dead, Hell Week was over. Roe and Schoons tenderly guided me down the hall to the shower room, and they kindly waited outside the stall to make sure I didn't fall down and split my head open or something. Next, they dressed me, muffled me up in coats and scarves, and aided me across the campus. The glare off the snow shredded my eyeballs and sent lightning streaking through my brain. I think the only sentence spoken during this whole time was, "Feels like you've got an ax stuck in your head, eh, Boomaga?"

I still felt awfully rocky during the initiation ceremony, but afterwards, at the banquet, I began to perk up and my head subsided substantially. By the time dessert came around, I found myself glowing with happiness and love, just as was everyone around me: last night was nagging only faintly at the back of my mind. And finally, when during coffee in the living room one of the brothers came up to me and with a sly wink said, "I hear you guys really threw a horror-show last night," I felt like hugging him. Damn tootin' we had thrown a horror-show the night before, and don't you forget it! I thought I never before had known such joy as that moment gave me.

In little less than a week's time, I had made rolling my way of living, and I had incorporated its vocabulary as a way of expressing that living. I found it not at all disagreeable to mix up a few "tinis, sours, or stumplifters" in a milk jug, jump into a "flip-top motivatin' unit," and "flazz off" in search of "furburgers." At first I "flailed" a good deal, taking the mythical "It" "in my ear" many

[53]

a time, but I gradually got the idea, learning how to "tip 'em up" more and "blow lunch" less; I learned to "rally" when mustering was called for; I learned to spend hours in the tube room "gooning at the box" and still pass my courses with acceptable grades; and I learned, with the advent of the "Bennie God" to make an acceptable "bennie-machine" out of aluminum foil, and use it on the flat back porch roof every afternoon during the spring semester to "catch a few rays" while downing some frosties. Though I never condoned public displays such as "throwing a gotcha," I soon came to be considered "Varsity Roller" material, and, if Schoons ever made the prediction that I would come around, it had, at last, come true.

Miracles of Miracles, when the dust settled in June, I had passed into my sophomore year: I packed up my new beer-soaked electric guitar on which I—the former esthetic classicist—had played nothing but E-A-B7 rock 'n' roll chords for three months, and went home.

Exhausted.

Yet in the fall, along with some other sophomores, I returned to school a week early, ostensibly to paint the house in preparation for rushing. At the end of the week we had completed but half the job, and, with college opening officially all around us, we took a break, carted six empty aluminum beer kegs, two trash barrels of beer cans and bottles, and several cases of unopened brew up from the bar to the back porch roof, and proceeded to bomb the submarine, a large boat-shaped gas tank which rested in the weeds close by the house. To do the job even more thoroughly, we unscrewed every lightbulb in the house and included them in the attack. Things got pretty wild, aided and abetted by the many cans of beer consumed during the bombardment, and I suddenly found myself hoisted into the air and used, in one final glorious barrage, along with several packs of cards, a china lamp, a brass cuspidor, a large clay sombrero ash-tray, three mattresses, some half-filled paint cans, and a bushel of rotten apples, to bomb the sub.

I landed on my back directly on top of the tank and bounced off into grass strewn with broken glass and other pointed projectiles. Observers said I should have been killed. As it was, I got up laughing. I gestured appropriately to my stunned audience above, walked out into the middle of the field behind the house, and passed out pleasantly beside last year's stock car which had run its last around that particular bit of ground, and now, wheelless, sank slowly into the ground. My body had not received a scratch. Nor my bones a chip.

Come around?—my God, I was a king! I gave up my life to one-hundred-per cent dissipation. I aimed myself high-wide-and-handsomely toward self-destruction!

CHAPTER THREE

ABOUT a month after being chucked off the roof, in the middle of an October Sunday morning, I was in the fraternity house library leafing through a magazine called *The Freshman Scoop,* a publication from a reasonably far, yet accessible, girl's college. Most colleges and universities in the East, both for men and women, have comparable magazines. Boy's schools get a hold of the girl's magazines; each fraternity most likely has a copy from every major school in its library with comments written in under the girls' pictures by the brothers— comments such as "likes to make," "frigid," "the picture does her too much justice," "box lunch," "a real roller," "get laid," ad infinitum. Sort of a rogue's gallery of who's getting it and who isn't and who could if he tried and who couldn't.

While leafing, I drank a cup of coffee, hoping this would salvage a blurred eyesight and minimize the pain in my head. I was also wondering when the Mickey Mouse would stop as it seemed I had been drunk or hung over ever since the incident of the sub. I was even definitely making up my mind to stay at school and grind the forthcoming weekend, as I had some very important hour

[56]

exams coming up. Being thus preoccupied, I almost missed Pookie's picture. In fact, I was about three pages by when it hit me that I'd passed a familiar face. I turned back and there she was. No mistake about it. Good old roll-'em Pookie. Glasses, scrubby hair, and all.

We—I, Roe, and Schoons—arrived at Pookie's school the following Saturday morning at seven after a grueling night trip in Schoons' '49 Oldsmobile called The Screaming Bitch which he had only recently transported from his home to school. He claimed the Bitch's transmission was lined with sawdust and the brakedrums with newspaper, and I, for one, believed him: she was unmistakeably the biggest heap on wheels. A milky gangrenous color, Schoons had further enchanced her beauty by painting in drippy fuschia letters on her either side: LIMPOPO VALLEY STUD FARM. Among her other attributes were exhaust fumes which she discharged with such energy through the front firewall, that just keeping the windows open wasn't enough to get rid of the poisonous fog—somebody had to constantly fan the right front door open and shut, and this, as we pulled to a stop that windy morning, was exactly what I'd been doing for four hours.

They had a dry campus, so we began winning votes right away when I opened the front door and three or four beer cans fell out and clattered down the sloping street. You wouldn't believe how loud a few beer cans can sound on a dry campus at seven-thirty in the morning. To make matters worse, when we had taken off from school at three in the morning after an eight hour marathon at the V.T., I had not forgotten to include my electric guitar and portable amplifier with the Bitch's cargo. We lugged the stuff onto the lawn in front of Pookie's house and assembled it: the guitar made an inhuman sound; I think the very foundations of the house trembled.

Thirty seconds later, there was Pookie on the front porch with a couple of other girls, all knuckling the sleep out of their eyes and looking none too pleased.

If I remember correctly, I was lying on my back strumming, the guitar resting on my belly. Roe and Schoons were playing Indians and wagon trains, whooping it up around me. It must have been quite a sight to see. Roe wore a thing on his head which you might have called an Australian Campaign Hat, though it couldn't hold a brim any longer for all the beer that had been dumped in and drunk out of it. He also wore a black jacket with a purple Bugs Bunny head on the back. Schoons was dressed—after a fashion—in a sweetshirt picturing a crudely inked but unmistakeable Adolf Hitler on the front, and a Howdy Doody on the back. Underneath Howdy Doody was written, once again in drippy fuschia letters: I AM A MUCKING FONSTER. Hockey gloves completed his outfit. Posed and pretty, relaxed and cool; leaves were swirling all around us.

Pookie checked her watch, I think to be sure it really was seven-thirty in the morning, then she screamed:

"Jerry Payne, you lop-eared lily-livered son of a double-crossing egg-laying mammoth, you shut up, God damn you, you and your God damn friends, you God damn animals, *shut up!*"

I stopped, Roe and Schoons stopped, the leaves stopped: only the big thud-a-duh echo of the guitar took a while to run down. Roe and Schoons collapsed; I bolted upright. Poking my fingers in my ears, I said, "For the luvva Mike, woman, don't shout so!"

Schoons thought this was the fuckin'-A twitty-bird funniest thing the Regals (Himself) had ever heard, and cackled accordingly, letting his bridgework fall out onto the lawn. The girls on the porch looked fit to kill; but they said not a word.

"Seriously, all kidding aside, we need shaves," I said, trying to sound little-boy sincere. "Does anybody have a razor?"

"The Regs'll take a grasshacker (lawnmower) and the fuzz (head) off a little green man (Ballantine Ale)," Schoons said. Without his teeth, his words came out in big doughy lumps; but nobody would have understood him anyway.

"You ought to get an interpreter for your monkey," Pookie said, motioning us reluctantly inside.

She borrowed razors and shaving cream for us, and we crowded into the downstairs hall john. Actually, what it was was a water closet. There wasn't room for one, let alone three guys to shave in there. Roe tried standing on the toilet lid and leaning over into the top of the mirror. He lost his balance twice and fell on my head each time. The second time he almost cut off my ear. Schoons said we were certainly lacking in couthness. Something in the way he said it set Roe to giggling, I joined him, and soon Schoons was hee-hawing louder than both of us. Then the door opened: it was Pookie looking at us like a thunder head ready to boom.

"Hope I'm not breaking anything up, boys," she said in a pleasant, lilting way, then dropped her voice to sub-zero, snapped her lips into a snarl, and hissed; "If you bullguano'd fetuses aren't out of here by the time I count ten!—"

Giggling intermittently, we cleaned up quickly and marched out into what we thought for sure would be a firing squad. But, amazingly, there was no housemother as yet present, and not one of the fifty girls glowering in our direction said a word except Pookie.

"You three jackasses can come to breakfast if you want," she said. I had a queer feeling that the girls were planning to make us the breakfast.

Unfortunately, we were served fried eggs. This set us to giggling and stabbing the yolks—"Yummy, yummy, fried cyclops eyes"—and we ate next to nothing. The other girls in the room riveted not us, but rather Pookie with knifelike stares. As if it were her fault!

"What brings you into this neck of the woods?" she asked me when I had quieted down some.

"We began celebrating last night," I explained. "We had this great party in honor of the death of the Bennie God. About three this morning, someone suggested we come here, and nobody could think of any reasons for not coming, so here we are."

"You must have bent over backwards to celebrate," she said. "You smell like last Sunday's upchuck."

"We tipped a few," I replied. "How are you?"

"What's all the sudden interest? You heard I was rich?"

"I'm sorry, honestly, Pookie. I'm a cad, a louse, a bounder, a rogue, a dastard; beat me over the head with a bull's pizzle but filch not from me my good name. How are you?"

She stared, then wiped her brow with her index finger,

snapped it in the air, and said, "Whew!" A smile began and died on her lips. "You've changed a lot, haven't you? At least, you don't make any bones about being grubbier, and oceans drunker..."

"You wouldn't know the kid," interrupted Schoons, pointing his fork at me, from the end of which dangled a shred of egg that looked like like a rubberized jellyfish: "Boomaga has seen the light; it's pierced his great ivory dome."

"The wild horses of wisdom stampede in his unencumbered brain," Roe asserted, flipping his egg onto its back. He began to smooth off the grease with the flat of his fork. When he noticed we were watching attentively, he explained; "I put 'em to sleep this way; then it doesn't hurt when I cut off their little heads," and he brought his knife harshly down on the yolk, dissecting it.

Meanwhile, Pookie turned to me. "There I was," she said, "up there snuggled tight in my bed in the midst of one of those early morning semi-conscious lazy dreams, really enjoying it, when suddenly everything began to shake and somebody grabbed my shoulder and I heard an hysterical female voice shouting 'Pookie, there's some crazy guys down there; Pookie, c'mon! One of them's setting up an electric guitar in the yard, a rock and roll guitar, help us stop him!' and I told whoever it was to be Evil-Eye McFleegle and go hit whoever was making the disturbance with a double-whammy or something, and the next thing I knew I was lying on the floor, so I got up and fell into some clothes, located my glasses, scratched a few pounds of web from my eyes, and descended as far as the front porch, where, lo and behold, I was confronted by..." She twirled her index fingers around each other,

[61]

then broke one away and jabbed it dramatically at me. "You know," she added; "even dressed in that filthy jacket, smelling to seventh hell of stale beer and cigarettes, you're still the skinny shaggy scruffy-looking grown-up version of The Kid in the Charlie Chaplin movie ... Do you have a Glorious beetle to show me this time?"

I said it was a Gloriosa, and no, I didn't happen to have brought one along.

"That's too bad," she said; "how did you find me?"

I explained about getting my hands on *The Scoop*.

"Does your friend here always eat with his hockey gloves on?" she next asked, indicating Schoons.

"Bet your sweet mams he does," Schoons replied, dropping his fork for the fifteenth time.

"Hobble-gobble remsin to you," Pookie said coldly. To me she said, "Now that you're here, what do you plan to do?"

"We were thinking along the lines of a gang-bang," Schoons said, adjusting his teeth with several unpleasant lip contortions.

Pookie stared at him, her eyes fogging up as if they were cold and somebody had suddenly breathed on them. Schoons wilted under her gaze, shrugged, and said, "So the Regals apologizes; so forget it."

"What are you planning to do?" Pookie asked me again.

I told her we had planned on nothing and everything; the sky was the limit.

"I think I'll go to my morning classes," she said.

"Heaven help us!" Roe exclaimed, throwing up his hands; "I guess that's hardly out of the question at all."

[62]

"Pookie," I argued; "there's a case of beer in the Bitch that has to be drunk, it's a beautiful day, so why don't you grab some of your friends and we'll have a party someplace?"

"You think after you three come in here I have any friends left?"

"You must have a couple of lagering buddies," Schoons pleaded.

"Oh, sure. A couple of lagering buddies: good grief!"

But she did. And we had a party: Schoons, Roe, Pookie, a friend of hers called Nancy Putnam, and another friend whom I don't remember very well except she was called Issimo or something and had a reputation for drinking people under the table, and myself. A mile out of town we turned off the highway and bumped over a dirt road that led to a popular parking spot on a knoll overlooking the local river. The girls fell out of the Bitch gagging, complaining of the smell, but once we'd pitched camp they cheered up. Beers were opened all around, and we lolled in the leaves, talking, drinking, relaxing.

Almost immediately the world became our oyster; we were six enlightened people whose arms could have encircled the universe, and the atmosphere of the day bouyed us up until, if we'd been challenged, I believe there would have been no one among us who would not have said he believed in his own immortality. We grew mellow; we grew oh so mellow. After his third beer, Schoons stood up and chucked his can between two trees into the river.

"Look at that old soldier go," he mourned. "Drifting with the tide. Adios, amigo mio ..." He rubbed his stomach and looked at the sky as if he had just noticed it was

[63]

there. Then he sat down and took off his fruitboots and socks, and wiggled his toes in the cool air. "Once a month they gotta breathe," he said.

We sat or lay in a kind of circle, the carton of brew in the center, a college-type campfire. And we talked. We talked of this and that—we talked of old rolls and friends who were graduated and in the army now or married; we talked of the political situation and dismissed it by deciding to hypdrogenically blow up Africa, Russia, China, Viet Nam, and South America. Then the talk degenerated into Little Moron jokes, and when the last clock had gone out the window for the purpose of seeing time fly, and the last straw had been fed to a nightmare, we took a break and lined up on the river bank, tossing our empties into the water. They bobbed and rolled; some sank, others were carried swiftly downstream out of sight.

"I wonder where they're all going?" Pookie mused.

"Out to sea," Roe said dreamily. "That's where I'd like to go—out to sea."

"We ought to build a raft," I said.

"What's there to make one out of?" asked the Issimo girl.

"Logs. There must be a lot of dead trees along the river bank," Roe suggested.

"We could tie them together and build a tent big enough to sleep six, and then buy this huge American flag..." Pookie was quite enthused.

"What about a cube unit?" Schoons asked.

"A what?"

"A refrigerator," I hastily explained to the uninformed.

"We can't send a raft down the flow without a unit," Schoons said, feigning great alarm.

"Sure. We can take all canned stuff," Pookie said.

"I suppose we put the frosties in a big net and drag 'em behind in the water?" Schoons said.

"Oh sure," Roe said. "A snag comes along, catches in the net, rips it open, and five hundred soldiers go down to Davey Jones' little locker. Nice work."

Schoons made such a face I thought for sure he had swallowed his teeth or something.

"Don't panic," Pookie said, "we'll take a refrigerator."

"Where you gonna plug it in?" the Issimo girl asked.

"Oh, God damn!" Schoons exclaimed. "Where we gonna plug it in, the skirt wants to know!"

"Why don't we plug it in Schoons'—"

"Stop!" Pookie yelled at me. "No filth!"

"Yes, Ma'am!"

But as luck would have it, Pookie's sudden taboo on filth only served to bring it on in droves. It was curious how we stood in a line, looking down into the river, recounting some of the grungiest jokes known to mankind, each in his own turn, including the girls, laughing— laughing until we were sitting, then laughing until we were scattered in various flung positions, gasping for breath, whooping and screaming while—once again for we boys—tears ran down our faces, and the girls, though red as beets, were laughing with us, all except Nancy Putnam who smiled and was bewildered by it all. When this session was over, we groped our way back to our former positions around the beer campfire, weak and happy, and the last of the warm lagers fizzed open at a rapid rate.

I was lying beside Pookie: she had a twig and was scratching designs in the wide dusty place before her.

"Do you ever get the sudden urge to go fishing?" she asked.

I replied that I always had the urge to go fishing, but chances rarely came my way.

"I wish we had a pole right now," she said. She smoothed over the dirt with her palm, and with her twig made a design like so:

"That," I said triumphantly, "is a Mitosifish going into its anaphase!"

"You must be kidding," she said incredulously. "Anyone can see it's nothing but a simple Spop."

"I give up," I said; "a what?"

"A Spop. Five minutes after they're born, they explode, so they live in more of a hurry than people, but not much more. I don't think we could ever catch a whole one, because by the time you can reel them in, there's only half of them left."

"Good Lord..."

She rubbed out the Spop and drew another fish:

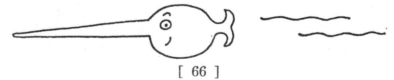

I, like a numbskull, suggested the obvious: a swordfish. I almost felt embarrassed under her scornful gaze.

"Jerry, you ought to know better than that. It's obviously a Long-Billed Sneet." She looked at me quizzically, waiting for suggestions as to the Sneet's habits, life cycle, etc.

"No, you go right ahead, Pookie; it's your baby." I began to feel dreamy. Leaves streaked by in the periphery of my vision. Pookie's stick added a meditative touch here and there to the Sneet, all very slow, very cottony.

"There are big Sneets, and very little Sneets," she explained. "The little Sneets live in small streams and come out onto golf courses at night. They drive their bills into the ground, and wait for someone to tee a golf ball on their tails..."

She quickly smoothed the earth, and drew a Sneet being a tee:

"But the sad thing is, nobody plays golf at night," she said almost moodily. "The Sneets wait there all night long, shining like gold coins in the spongy grass, hoping against all hope that a golfer will come along, but one never does. You see they're so delicate they can't come out during the day when the sun would set them afire. Once in a very rare while, however," she added, drawing again, "a very small cold star will float down and sit on their tails for a while. It makes them quite happy."

"And what about the big Long-Billed Sneets?"

"Oh, they have a different problem," she said, filling the star full of dots. "They're very amorous and they love to kiss, but they have a devil of a time doing it. They have to approach very slowly so that their tips meet, which is almost impossible because any slight current moves them up or down or to the side since they don't have any fins or flippers to stabilize themselves. And if after a long struggle they ever do get a perfect touching of their billtips, they're too tired to really enjoy it." She squibbled up the dirt with the twig, snapped the twig in half, then quarters, and tossed the bits at my head. "Would you like to go for a sort of a walk along the riverbank?" she asked, after the last twig-bit had bounced off my cheek.

"Why not . . . ?"

We informed the others that we would be right back, and left. We walked a ways in silence: the wind blew Pookie's hair so that isolated sections would flip up, then be blown instantly flat, like new wings just learning life. On our left there were trees stretching along the top of the riverbank; on our right there was a field of low brown stubble that spread for acres and acres to an almost invisible barb wire fence.

"You know, Jerry," Pookie said in a quiet voice; "one

hundred years from now I'm going to be able to remember the stuff that was bubbling out of our minds today. One hundred years from now I bet I'll have a dream that will come to me as often as I want it to, a dream of a raked pile of our pretty metaphors, and the wind swooping down upon it, scattering the metaphors like cheap agates across the fields and mellowing valleys where they will come to rest glittering nervously, a crop of small rootless prisms waiting to be pecked up and swallowed by flocks of enormous dark Arthurian corbies ... Write that down for posterity, will you, Jeeves? I intend to lead a very quotable life.'' She wasn't looking at me; she was staring up at the clouds; up at the wind, the sky.

"So how did it happen?" she asked suddenly.

"How did what happen?"

"Your transformation."

"What do you mean my—"

"Into this filthy glopular beastie that drives around in heaps of tin painted to look like rotten cabbages," she said.

"Oh—that."

"The ivory dome," she said brightly, tapping her head.

"I don't know; it just sort of happened ..."

"Tell me about it."

So I told her about rushing, about being lamped with uncalled for regularity, about Poopsick whom I'd grown rather fond of now that he was a big dog, housebroken, and no longer under my care, about Hell Week, about the Scavenger Hunt, and about being used to bomb the sub.

"Do they give you a number?" she asked when I was through.

"A number? What for?"

"So they can tell who you are."

"I don't get it."

"Oh ... I don't either." She took off her glasses and ahed on the lenses, then bent and polished them on the hem of her skirt. "How would you like to hear about me?" she said pertly, sliding the glasses back on and stretching her eyes a couple of times to settle them once more into the myopic groove.

Before I could answer yes or no, she had launched into the Life And Hard Times Of Pookie Adams from the time of her last letter to the present moment.

Once out of the hospital, she had returned to school, gone through the folderol of being stared at and whispered over, and had at last graduated by the skin of her wit. Frankly speaking, however, her graduation from high school was no great success. It rained all that day so the ceremony was moved inside to the gymnasium. When the organ stopped playing, her very crotchety father treated them all—her mother, herself, Uncle Bob, and Aunt Marian—to sundaes at a Howard Johnson, after which they went home. Pookie trundled up to her room and lay down on the bed, where she spent three hours pulling the ring in her teddy bear's head, tapping time to the song with her bare feet against the wall. Her room was empty, no pennants tacked along the molding, no dance cards or old corsages pinned to the lampshade, no football letter sweaters hanging around, no nothing. She had a cork bulletin board for snapshots, but there was only one: herself standing on a dock holding a small bass she had just caught. Joe Grubner had taken the picture at his father's summer place. Good Old Dead Joe Grubner.

And there she was at the end of a long organized schooling—life, really—wondering what the hell had been good or bad, but she couldn't recall a thing, not even the day of her one solitary fish picture. Things were tough all over. There was nothing to do but sit on her bed and howl "Dromedary-romedary-omedary-medary-edary-dary-ary-ry-y ..." as loud as she could.

Her father came running up the stairs, tried the handle to the locked door, and then shouted: "Pookie; for goodness sakes, what's the trouble?"

She replied; *"Monkey balls!"*

There was a shocked silence during which she could hear his ear stethescoping against the door.

"Pookie, dear; you should unlock the door, please."

"Hell, thunder, and damnation I should!"

His feet shuffled away, hesitated, and returned. She waited until she was sure his lower jaw was in the act of dropping downward for the purpose of saying something, then she shouted:

"Fuzzy wuzzy wuz a bear, so there!"

On that note, he retreated from the field of battle. And Pookie was alone. Rain plip-plopped against the window; rain drizzled drearily over everything. She went to the window and, to her surprise, observed the same miniscule world captured in fifty different rain drops. It was beautiful. So she drew back her fist and let the window have it. Even that was disappointing because she only cut herself on one knuckle (she showed me a small white scar). And she couldn't cry because her tear ducts were constipated.

Once too often she pulled the teddy bear's ring; it broke and refused to play. That did it! With a pair of

[71]

scissors she cut the bear's mechanical heart out, and followed up by stabbing her pillow to death, scattering the feathers helter-skelter over the room. She dumped all her books on the floor, then cleaned her butterfly and insect collection, stamping it into a jeweled oblivion of cotton, bright pieces of wings, and splinters of glass. Chaos obtained, she bolted from the house, ran straight up to the Tadpole Pond, and waded into the middle where the water only came to her waist. The damn thing had certainly shrunk since her frog-skewering days! She splashed around a bit, getting good and covered with mud, but traipsed home feeling a little better. Her parents were shocked, though true to form they refrained from prolonged comment. They lovingly tucked her into bed after a shower and some beef boullion.

But by the end of the abjectly idle summer, she was ready for college, nametagged from the top of her head to her toes, as scrubbed and polished and well-wished as a cloud's silver lining; and also undeniably excited. For college was going to be the new life: capital NEW, capital LIFE. She had made up in her cacophonous little mind a land where bells rang every hour, sending historical ghosts scrambling across the golden ivy facades of burnt brown buildings, while comradely laughter bubbled deep in the well shadows of trim New England glens. And when she finally arrived she let out an horrendous war whoop and jumped up to catch a large yellow leaf as it was blown by. She caught the leaf, but fell off the train platform in the process, nearly busting every bone in her body. But so what?—she'd never been so elated in her life!

Her elation carried over into the first couple of weeks,

and before she knew it she had a good friend. ("Me who had up to that time lived on a small planet inhabited by friendly will-o-the-wisps, gremlins, flibbertigibbets, banshees, poltergeists, kelpies, and what have you; everything except people ...") The girl was her roommate, Nancy Putnam, and the college personality-interest machine had cast them together, one of the few times, perhaps, it hadn't forecast wrong, and with one of its most difficult cases to boot.

Nancy was (as I could plainly see) a quiet girl with a feathery smile, trusting and simple and healthy looking, a sort of whimsical Shirley Temple, or a blond Breck Shampoo girl (if I was familiar with the ads, which I wasn't). About the fourth day, Nancy suggested they take a walk, so take a walk they did.

They meandered south out of town, turned off the highway onto an interesting seldom-traveled artery, and followed it a ways. There were pastures on either side dotted with idle cows. At one point, they halted beside a barb wire fence. A cow sashayed over to have a gander at them, stopping not more than two feet away. It looked very wise, sleepily grand, and—probably for the girls' benefit—it had ceased chewing its cud. They sized each other up for a few minutes, until Nancy said:

"Wouldn't it be great if cows could talk?"

"What do you mean?"

"Oh ... take this one for instance. It absolutely looks as if it were about to say something, perhaps 'Hello, I'm Joe, your friendly neighborhood milkman.' It would be great, wouldn't it, if it could come right out and say it, and we could reply ... oh ..."

"Something like 'Why, Hello, Joe, we're your friendly

neighborhood butchers.' " Pookie said, and they both laughed, stuck out their tongues at the grave moonface on the other side of the fence, and ran away.

After that incident, they moseyed along the road some more, chewing on a weed here, kicking a pebble there, humming snatches of songs, and generally enjoying themselves. Eventually they came to rest on a grassy spot beneath a tree where they chatted idly for a while, then drifted into a discussion of life. Nancy handed Pookie an over-all view similar to looking into one of those pink crystaled Easter eggs with a window, quaint and very breakable, something you want to put on a shelf for all time, even though you know it will go stale, probably rot if the ants don't get to it first. It pained you, you wanted to attack it, destroy it, but you refrained for the same reason you didn't expose Santa Claus to little kids: some of their belief was always rubbing off on you. Innocence —the powdered sugar on a doughnut.

"And you want to know something?" Pookie said, skipping ahead of me. "You want to know how I feel about life now?"

"Go right ahead..."

"I feel like..." her words were blown back at me like bright leaves; "I feel like there's a great big beautiful something for *me*, and it's right on the tip of my heart waiting to explode. Like an almost-but-not-quite climax when you're positively electrified with rhythm, about to bust open big and red and glorious as a bomb, whamo! raining silver bullets of flesh over the entire world, and then when it just tickles around the detonator and doesn't go off, boy-oh-boy do you ever get frantic, know what I mean? You feel it's just got to happen..." She turned

[74]

around and stopped, hands on her hips, legs spread defiantly.

"Hallelujah!"

"Oh ... you know what you can do ..." She attacked and tried to push me over the steep bank into the river. I grabbed her arm and swung her around so that our positions were reversed and her back was to the water.

"Any last words?"

"Kiss me before I die." She lifted her lips.

I balked.

"Same old Jerry, eh? What are you afraid of: syphilis? hoof and mouth disease? ha?"

"If you were good-looking or stacked or something, I would," I retaliated. "But who wants to kiss something that looks like a Korean orphan? I feel sorry for you, I want to give you some bread."

She actually threw herself backwards: if I'd let go I'm sure she would have tumbled down the bank. I was hard put to keep her in tow.

"I want to drown!" she yelled, pretending ferociousness. "You beast! Let me die!"

"No!"

"Help, help! I'm being ravaged!"

"Shuttup!"

"Why?"

"Because."

"Because, because, because!"

Wildly flailing her arms, she threw me off balance, and we crashed to earth atop the rise, I more or less spread-eagled over Pookie. Stammering "excuse me's" a mile a minute, I did a fast awkward pushup. But for a second our eyes had been close enough to seem double: the moment that followed was very quiet. Lying side by side we stared down at the river where liquid sunlight streamed along surface eddies, describing the merging and flowing of currents.

"I don't think drowning would be so bad." Pookie's voice was quite matter-of-fact.

Searching for something casual to say, I said; "It's quicker than liquor."

She agreed. "And so much more enjoyable. Especially on a day like this. The water would look like it was full of spoons—small silver spoons—that would glint above my head and just beyond the tips of my fingers. I'd probably float down the river way below the surface on my back, and above me I would be able to see the cow muzzles looking like harmonicas with their flabby lips wrinkled back to drink, and maybe I would even see the long starched stomachs of crocodiles sunning themselves, and then there would be a long soapy stretch where all the mothers would be washing..."

"And then there would be a big grappling hook," I said.

"You're a nice guy. Who are you, the original iconoclast?"

"But that's what would happen," I insisted.

"What *would* happen doesn't count," she said.

"I see: it only counts when your team scores the basket."

"Exactly."

"Big Rock Candy goof-off."

"Exactly."

"A bunch of baloney."

"Exactly."

I ran out of epithets, so I said, "Let's go back; that beer must be getting lonely."

"With your friends around? They don't drink beer, they rape it!"

That tickled my fuzzy. It was so funny, that as we got up I impetuously grabbed her hand and we began to run back. But I'm no athlete: after thirty yards, I slowed us huffing and puffing to a walk. Or at least I was huffing and puffing.

"Come on, come on; don't quit now," Pookie urged excitedly. "Let's race. Last one back is a rotten egg!"

"Then I'm—puff, puff—a—puff—rotten egg."

"You can't be that out of shape."

"Shape ... dear girl ... is something ... I was never in."

"Well, I'm going to run back without you, then."

"You're entirely welcome to; bon voyage."

"First you have to let go of my hand."

"Oh ... hand." I let it drop. But she didn't leave right away; she pleaded some more."

"Come on, Jerry; running's good for you. It builds strong bodies twelve ways." She planted herself in front of me, hands once again defiantly on her hips. I had to stop.

"It may be good for you, but not for me," I said.

"You know what's going to happen, don't you? You're going to grow up and be nothing but a big basketball of flesh. Somebody will have to wheel you around on a bed. Your muscles will all atrophy. Your stomach will be distended from too much beer. You'll be a vegetable, a great big blob-like fungus with mushrooms sprouting out of

[77]

your ears, that's what's going to happen. Aren't you at all concerned?"

"Not a mite."

"All right for you, then." She thumbed her nose at me. "You're the rottenest egg of all, Jerry Payne!"

"Yay, rah-rah, rottenest egg of all!"

But she didn't run away. She danced. With an exhilarating slow motion, leaping softly into the autumn air almost as if there were no gravity, or so I saw her then. Sometimes her face was turned to me, laughing, inviting me to come too; sometimes she was turned away, leaning forward or bending, her arms flung limply into the air like long white wings, looking for all the world as if she were floating.

"Rotten egg," came back to me: "Jerry Payne's a rotten egg!" At last she shouted "Phooey!" and sprinted away, diminishing along the edge of the field. I suddenly wished, pain or no, that I were beside her running, but of course, it was too late: just as I had broken into an undecided jog, she swerved off to the side out of sight to where the others were drinking.

"Hey..." I whispered; "hey, Pookie..." the path before me was far and empty; "hey, Pookie...I love you..."

It wasn't the way she would have wanted it—a great three-day hike across the cruel wide country, a gauzy moonlit handkerchief fluttering down upon us, a long singing time in the sweet fluorescent light of night-blooming cotton fields—but what the hell...? It happened, didn't it?

CHAPTER FOUR

IT HAPPENED, all right. In fact, it happened so badly I found myself visiting Pookie nearly every weekend. Most often I journeyed to her college alone on a bus, because love was something very new and not for one minute did I want the likes of Roe and Schoons messing up my romantic weekends. Overnight I became—once again—a new man; a non-roller, a lover. The brother inebriates worried about me for a week or two, undeniably saddened that one of their members should so suddenly go to ruin over a skirt.

"Boomaga," said Schoons early one morning, leaning over my bed and asphyxiating me with his breath after having damn near kicked my door down on his entrance; "love is candy-ass, it don't mean squat." I could tell his teeth were missing by the potato shape of his words.

"What would you know about it?" I asked him.

"The Regals knows," he said, tipping backwards and fortunately landing in a chair. There he sat, breathing heavily, conjuring up a thought in the darkness. All he said finally, was, "The Kid's been there."

"Look; why don't you leave me alone?" I begged. "I need my beauty sleep."

[79]

"Ronnie says 'Where's Boomaga?' He wants to know is he dead or what?"

"Next time you see him tell him I'm dead, okay?"

Schoons panted some more, and, though I couldn't see very well, I knew he was blinking his eyes rapidly, a sure sign that he was trying to think. After a moment he said, "She doesn't even have a pair of decent jugs!"

"Jugs," I haughtily replied, "aren't everything."

"Nor is she a looker!"

I explained that looks weren't everything either.

"I suppose she's a real gunner; bangs away, huh?"

"Schoons, you better watch it; I'm going to punch you out ..."

"But Boomaga," he pleaded; "how can a guy stand aside twiddling his phalangos, and watch his bosom buddy take a flying douche? I created you with my own hands, I nursed you with tender loving care towards the pap of your first mellow malt, and what do I get for thanks ...? Head over tea kettle for a flip-top box ..."

"I appreciate your concern," I said; "where are your teeth?"

"Ronnie's keeping 'em down at the bar. I broke 'em ..." he moaned glumly.

"In a fight?" But he was asleep, expelling enormous black clouds of halitosis with every exhalation. I got up and opened the window; how could I ever hope to explain to him, or for that matter to anyone, the Great Spiritual Evolution going on in my humble body?

It was a very happy time: as Pookie sometimes called it—a Nightingale Time, a time of singing. Regularly on Friday evenings around eight, my bus pulled into the depot, and invariably as I stepped out of the bus, Pookie was there, not five feet away, the collar of her polo coat turned up, her arms crossed for warmth, her breath frosty plumes disappearing into the chill night air. Even though the bus was seldom less than an hour late, she never complained: she ate Baby Ruths and played the pinball machine in the grubby depot until I arrived. Then, as my foot touched the ground, she smiled a huge smile, took off her glasses, and rushed to give me a good long kiss, not particularly to the delight of the people getting off behind me, who squeezed awkwardly around us muttering dark oaths, their bags bumping against our legs. But who cared?—certainly not us. We kissed, touching tongue tips, squeezing as close together as our heavy coats would allow us, for all the world like a couple of movie stars. And that first kiss was always a knockout: I felt after it as if, after a long day spent exercising in the snow, I had come inside, and, with my boots off and an old fashioned in my hand, I was sleepily gazing into the sunset flames of a thick fire. Downright woozy, lazy, and ecstatic, you might say: or something along that line.

When we came up for air, Pookie said, "Check your bag, sir?" and wrested the overnight satchel from my hand. Then, hand in hand, we walked down the hill from the depot along the main street, Pookie swinging the satchel in huge windy circles while she enthusiastically recounted the episodes of her week, and cross-examined me for news of mine. Thus we walked, always on the left hand side of the street, on smoky October nights, on still November nights, on snowy December nights.

There were several clothing stores, a sporting goods store, a toy store, and a gift shop along the way: we had to stop in front of each to discover what was new in the window since the last time we had passed by. I was never much good at this, but Pookie was a champ. In the clothing stores new dresses, sweaters, ski togs, and what have you came and went with vertiginous speed; in the sports shop fencing foils regularly replaced boxing gloves; in the toy store windup Santa Clauses replaced plastic pilgrims; and in the gift shop—the best of them all— each week a new hand-carved, hand-painted New Englandish sea captain or bar wench was added to a long line of wooden dolls that stretched almost the width of the window. And of course, each week one of the characters Pookie especially liked was gone.

Noticing how much she loved these figurines, I splurged for Christmas and damn near bought out the store for her. It was the first present I ever gave to a girl. I made the purchase on a Saturday morning and took this big bag full of goodies with me to her house. I was sitting at the piano trying to act nonchalant, when she came back from her classes and sat down beside me on the bench, books in her lap. I gave her the bag, mumbling awkwardly about "Merry Early Christmas," then played some dinky tune while she dug into the bag and pulled out the first one. I remember from out the corner of my eye how she unrolled the white tissue from it, how startled she was, then how she smiled, took off her glasses, kissed me on the cheek, and set the gift on top of the keys. There must have been eight or ten of them lined up from middle C to high E when Pookie had finished unwrapping, and she could only shake her head, saying "But why all at once?" and "I love you" in the same breath. I can safely say that gift was one of the biggest thrills of my life.

Well, so: we walked down the street from the depot.

In the center of town, it was our custom to stop in at a Friendly's for a hot chocolate. The seats in there were so low Pookie said we were actually in a doll's house, and I must admit it was rather disconcerting to find your head at fly-level of those who were serving you. But it was a popular place with the college crowd; it had a bright, sort of steamy atmosphere. Pookie always paid for the hot chocolate; it was understood to be her treat. In fact, many places we went, whether out to dinner, to dance, or to drink, she often insisted we at least go dutch.

"I think it's ridiculous for the boy to pay all the time," she said. "It makes it uncomfortable for him, and uncomfortable for me, because suppose I want to drink like a fish or eat like a pig and I think 'Gee, does Jerry have enough money? Should I drink beer instead of a Manhattan? Should I have a hamburger instead of a steak?' That's ridiculous. So we go dutch, and everybody eats and drinks what he wants and no hard feelings, and if you suddenly think your masculinity's getting sheared off, just say so, and I'll let you pay." How can you argue with reasoning like that?

Emerging from Friendly's warm and complacent, we took a side street to the boarding house where Pookie had beforehand reserved a room for me. It was the same house every time, a miniature Victorian structure, and each room resembled the next—nothing more than a bed, a wash basin, a night table, and a chair. The landlady, a stout, wiry-haired widow who used a lorgnette and who didn't give much of a hoot about respectability, raised no fuss when Pookie remained in my room with the door closed (and locked) for upwards of an hour. These were our passion periods, spent more or less fully clothed on the bed, feeling each other up and what have you. My awkwardness—that is, my timidity—under pressure greatly retarded our lovemaking, but at least I was not as bad as that night on the bus when we first met. I have to laugh now when I think of us under the covers of one of those cool white beds—I fully clothed but for my jacket, tie, and shoes; Pookie likewise dressed but for her sweater and loafers—going through the official fornicating motions until, inevitably, I wet my pants and that was that. At the time, however, each new progress and each sterile climax seemed like earth's end to me, and I never heard Pookie really complain. Thinking about it now, I am a little surprised she didn't suggest that we cut out the hanky-panky, strip down, and get it over with. I guess she wanted me to suggest it, and she bore up remarkably well under my fumbling onslaught.

Other than myself, there was another reason partially responsible for why the consumation of our love affair was delayed—time: we had very little of it on those Friday nights. One evening we prolonged our thrashing longer than usual, with the result that Pookie was half an hour late for her check in. After that incident, she always showed up at the bus station with an alarm clock in her pocket. I came to abhor the infernal machine. It sat on the bedside table tick-tocking away while we made out, and never failed to ring at exactly the moment I myself was going off, leaving me to lie face down, draining my passion against nothing, while Pookie dashed around the room searching for shoes, coat, sweater, gloves, or what have you, and then—blowing me a kiss— ran out the door, shouting something over her shoulder about when we should meet tomorrow. I don't think she ever forgot to take the clock with her; if she had, I would certainly have bought a hammer and smashed it to powder.

Tomorrows—that is, Saturday mornings—were lazy and fun, undirected and unimportant. I woke up around ten, and, after a hot breakfast at the boarding house, walked to Pookie's house where I sat in the foyer reading magazines or plinking out tunes on the piano. When she returned from her morning classes around eleven we sat out the time until lunch reading newspapers together, playing cards, or perhaps fingering out duets on the piano. The cards quite often turned into games of fifty-two pick-up, and duets occasionally evolved into fist-banging fiascos which brought reprimands from the house mother or the house president or someone: but by and large we were tolerated because we were very happy: "Dirigible big and light," Pookie called us.

Saturday afternoons were spent viewing art shows, or sniffing flowers in the campus greenhouses, or talking in some popular café over mugs of chocolate and coffee, or simply going for long walks. I suppose we walked millions of miles in those days. Pookie had a special thing about walking: she wanted to make some hollow-soled shoes with holes in the bottom that would steam out a scarlet paint at every footstep. Then when she was old, she would go very high up in a plane and look down to see her footsteps traveling over the earth, looking like the dyed important cells on a slide of otherwise grey matter. "Footsteps are too damn incognito," she complained.

Be that as it may, I can picture us easily against backgrounds of leaves, stark countryside, and snow, walking, always walking, setting down our size 5's and 9's that, as soon as we lifted our feet, no longer existed: and nothing startling happened; there were no big events that would stand forever as monuments to our lives.

Saturday nights were occupied by good dinners at the best tavern in town. They were long, candlelit affairs in a colonial setting: powder gourds, muskets, beaded pouches—you name it—hung from the hand-hewn ceiling beams; fox hunting prints and conscription posters from the Revolutionary and Civil Wars adorned the walls. We ate well, murmuring through our food, and dull candle flames burned in Pookie's glasses. It never occurred to me to ask her to take off those glasses, and it bothered her not a whit to wear them, although she could see fairly well, though very fuzzily, without them.

"Some girls go around blind, just so their dumb boy friends won't see them in their glasses," she once said. "What the hell's the difference? Have you ever seen anything sadder than a girl, who, after a year of going out with some guy, meekly confesses to him that she really does wear glasses? Yetch!"

Well...maybe we went to a dance after dinner. It was a favorite trick of Pookie's at these dances to shed her shoes and step on my feet, letting me move us around the dance floor. Often we spent whole evenings in this way and I never tired of it. Afterwards, of course, there was the devil to pay locating her shoes, as she never remembered behind which radiator or under which table she had thrown them.

If not to a dance, we went to a movie, or perhaps we contented ourselves with a few drinks in a bar until Pookie's curfew. Whatever we did, it was relaxed. I am constantly amazed to think that there was such a smooth time in our relationship. How is it possible that we went through five months or more hardly ruffling each other's feathers?

Then: Sunday. Sundays always came, and in the morning we often went to church with Nancy Putnam who was a devout Episcopalian. Mostly we went for a lark, and we thoroughly angered Nancy by deriding the services. She said we were heathens, and she was the most furious she was capable of being when both Pookie and I, who had never been confirmed, blithely partook of wafers and wine when offered the chance. "You've got to get something for your money," Pookie said, but Nancy didn't see it that way. So far as I know, mocking the church was the only thing that could even make the color rise in her face.

Church over, the weekend ostensibly was also. I dined at Pookie's house, and back we walked, first to the boarding house to get my things, then to the depot, Pookie once more in command of my bag, but this time holding it gloomily at her side. The bus was late nine times out of ten, so we often concluded the weekend to the banging and clanging of the pinball machine.

Then I was on the bus and leaving again, waving through a hole in the frosted green window, the sensation of Pookie's kiss still on my lips. All the way back, instead of reading an assignment, I thought about her, and as soon as I got back to school, instead of going straight to work, I wrote her a long letter, posting it that same night to be sure she would get it by Tuesday.

It was then only a question of whether I could survive until Tuesday, when Pookie's long letter to me would arrive. I actually cut biology lectures for months because they ran from nine to ten, Tuesdays and Thursdays, and the mail showed up at the fraternity house between nine-twenty and quarter of ten. If there were a holiday, or if for some reason the letters didn't arrive on time, I fretted myself blue and stamped around in a bad temper all the day long.

Taking all this into consideration, plus granting that the human body (and its eventual lack of patience) is what it is, it became progressively inevitable as the weeks rolled by that I would overcome my fear of downright grassroots sex, and I did. The long awaited-for day arrived when I wrote to Pookie and timorously suggested that the time had come, and was she in favor of a certain project? She sent a telegram in reply:

YOU BET I AM!

I crumpled up the telegram, and, wondering what the hell I had gotten myself in for, I became blissfully afraid.

Thus it was that I got laid for the first time in my life in February of that new year, approximately four hours after the Winter Carnival hockey game. I had bought my first packet of contraceptives, even practiced getting one of the damn things on if you can imagine that, but, prepared as I was, and with Pookie's one hundred per cent cooperation, I still damn near blew it from the word go.

My heart began beating right from the moment we stepped out of the hockey rink into the snowblown night well on our way toward being preserved in ice for all time. The temperature had been announced once over the loudspeaker during the game: fifteen below zero. Pookie's aplomb under such disquieting conditions was disconcerting: she was talking a blue streak about the game as if nothing at all were going to take place in the next few hours. She said she wished all the time that we were being frozen that she could have been down on the ice, not necessarily fiddling with the puck, but, oh to be able to curve and spin and dip, shine and flash in bursts of such awkward immaculate motion, and to be buffeted by the crowd's hysterical roar, its thirst for blood. She wanted to know if I had noticed one boy from the visting team, almost a midget, with dark retreating eyes and a bandage covering one cheek, who scored three or four times, and who, after each goal, raised his stick in the air, and, gliding smoothly away from the sprawled goalie and embarrassed defensemen, grinned half-toothlessly at the drunk and grumbling crowd.

I honestly thought she was nuts talking like that with what was ahead. I guess I was as eager as a guy can be who's been held down for nineteen years, but like I said, I was scared witless and saw no reason for her not to be also. Whatever, we stomped through the shifting drifts to where I had parked our wheels for the evening—who else but the Screaming Bitch? Schoons (being dateless, and there being several kegs on tap at the house) had generously loaned her to me. She was in worse shape than the previous fall: no heat, the wipers didn't work, the brake pedal went to the floor fifteen times before something grabbed, and to top things off, the headlights blew every five minutes; you had to grab a fuse from the supply in the glove compartment, jump out into air that froze your tonsils, and jam the fuse into its little slot over the regulator, then hope it would last for another five minutes before fizzling again. And of course there was the

[89]

smog problem; "A refrigerated tomb on wheels," Pookie said.

I knew all this before we started, but I was pretty sure I could handle it okay.

We skidded into a snowbank in front of Jack's All-Nite Mart on Route 16 and bought a loaf of French bread to go with the bottle of red wine I had bought a couple of days ago for the occasion. Then, with Pookie behind the wheel and me pushing against the hood, we should have backed out of the bank. Instead, the car jumped forward and drove me half way to China in snow.

"Put the God damn thing in reverse!" I shouted.

"That's where it is!" she shouted back.

I came around to check: she was right, that's where it was.

"You look like a human snowball," she said, tittering some.

"Let's try 'er again," I mumbled, staving off panic brought on by visions of a night spent in getting out of snowbanks.

This time we succeeded; I took the wheel and headed into a blizzard. We skidded, did a 360, slewed to one then the other side of the road, and stalled. I started her up again and the lights went out. I put in a new fuse, came back, and blew on my hands for a few minutes. Suddenly I noticed the air inside the Bitch was awfully thick. So I hollered at Pookie to keep the door flapping.

"But it's cold!" she complained.

Was it ever, and I, in typical fashion, had forgotten my gloves. We churned along, quickly freezing to death, and I had more visions, this time of Schoons seated complacently in a warm womb-like corner of the bar, sleepily bloating himself with beer.

"I bet they don't find our bodies until the spring thaw," Pookie griped, slamming the door shut and refusing to pump it any more. Faced with this mutiny I was ready to give up; I was ready to aim us at a snow drift, slump down behind the wheel, and let winter take its course.

Yet I didn't, and after getting lost three times; after getting stuck in another snowbank; after I had slipped on some ice while trying to dig us out again and slid under the car where I destroyed my head against the muffler; after all this, we chanced upon the right road and drew to a stop at our destination—The Kozy-Kabins of legendary fame. I was hardly rag'd at all.

"You look frazzled to a stub and twice as crotchety," Pookie said. "Come on, cheer up."

We sat quietly in the Bitch for a few minutes calming down. The windows steamed up and froze. I bowed my head against the steering wheel and pretended to bawl. Pookie rubbed the back of my neck. "Your hair is all white and stiff," she said; "just as if you'd run head-on through a wall of cotton candy."

"Somebody up there hates me," I said. I honestly felt like crying. It had taken us two hours to drive four miles.

"I can't disagree with that," Pookie said.

Then I became very sinister and calm, and had an attack of sarcasm aimed at Schoons, whose cozy form in its uteral corner had once again passed before my eyes. "By gosh," I said, "I love this car. This is the best old dadgummed car I was ever in. Shucks, if good old Harry Schoonover was to come up to me right now and say 'Jer, Old Boy, you give me a thousand bucks and this little

[91]

dandy's yours,' I'd break my golly all Jehosophat frozen neck reaching for my wallet. I'd even insist on paying an extra grand just because he was such a nice guy to offer it to me in the first place on the one very minor condition that I gas it up. Why, golly gee-whiz, I'd even do a dance. I'd run across campus in my underwear. I'd kiss good old Harry Schoonover smack-dab in his withered left ear, I would!''

"Okay, okay," Pookie said. "Let's abandon the snickering igloo to the tempest. You register with the Sloppy Joe that runs the place, and let's take our big rusty key and crawl into our room at the Ritz and collapse."

And we did. It wasn't a palace.

"Ladies and Gentlemen, let me describe for you the scene," Pookie nasled, holding her balled-up fist inches in front of her lips as if it were a microphone. "You are in an abandoned trapper's shack high in the Rocky Mountains. Listen to the wolves." She held her hand towards me; I gave an unspirited up-down whistle. "Wind is piping through the walls," she continued; "fine particles of snow are sifting in on the wind—like sandblasting. Much snow already lies like spilt sugar on the bed. And the bed, ah, the bed, Ladies and Gentlemen: a curiosity worth noting in itself. Imagine if you can a mattressish thing almost as large as the room, amply pummeled by generations of adolescent fornicators who are responsible for the spread being so bumpy it resembles a papier mâché relief map of the Himalayas. At the foot of this monstrosity, pedestaled on a small wooden table, is a television set. The rabbit ears on this set have been twisted and bent together into the shape of an idiotic heart by some former sadistic occupants. On the other side of the bed is a chair, behind the chair a door, behind the door most likely is a can. And Jesus-H.-Bullguano-Christ, where's the heat?''

She sat down on the only chair; I turned on the tube. I stood leaning against the foot of the bed checking out an old Franchot Tone movie until I remembered the wine. I'd forgotten a corkscrew so I had to dig out the cork with the car keys. It took me a while but I finally jammed the last piece of cork into the bottle. We ate bread and drank wine and chewed on little pieces of cork (''Corkettes'' Pookie called them) until most of the wine was gone, and Franchot Tone had ended, and even the Star Spangled Banner had been played. I couldn't think of any way to stall further so I said, ''I guess we might as well get ready for bed now if you want to or anything.''

''If I want to or anything!'' she exclaimed, her eyes sparkling. ''Jerry Payne, I was just wondering if I ought to shuck my loafers, break off my toes, and put them into a jar of formaldehyde or something for old time's sake! You know—P. Adams, Her Toes? It's about time!''

''It's about time,'' I repeated vaguely.

''Bro-ther.'' She got up and advanced toward me. ''You look as if, backed against an adobe wall freckled by bloody bullet holes, facing a bearded line of Cuban militiamen, you have just taken a last cigarette from the pack offered to you by some Captain Gonzalez. Well, Cape-ee-tan Gonzalez,'' she said, throwing her arms around my neck, ''no matter how you look at it you're a dead pigeon.'' Then she stepped back and said; ''You're scared.''

I shrugged. Don't sweat the small stuff.

''All right. Then I'll tell you what we're gonna do. You get to peel the tomato.''

"I what?"

"You get to strip me. You can do it as slow as you want, I don't care. Our object is to get you used to naked female bodies. The same way you get used to a new room, or a new model car; you have to look at it for a while." She smiled but she seemed nervous too. "Begin with the socks."

"Pookie, it's awfully cold in here . . ."

"Look, what do you want, Jerry? Do you want we should play peek-a-boo? Do you want you should close your eyes and promise not to peek and I should jump out of my clothes and into a big woolly nightgown, and then I should run for the bathroom, only you should have to stick your fingers in your ears so you wouldn't hear a thing, and then you should have to put your hands over your eyes again while I run out and jump under the covers, and then I should have to put *my* hands over *my* eyes while you undress, and *my* fingers in *my* ears while you're in the head . . . ? A lot of good all that would do us. No, it seems to me the only thing is to be natural and if we can't be natural right off the bat, well, let's just go at it in some kind of way that will bring us to be natural in the shortest time possible. Does that sound like a good idea to you? Begin with the socks, then . . ."

She sat on the bed while I took off her knee socks. Socks off, she stood up and outstretched her arms while I fiddled with the string under her chin that tied the hood of her parka. "I can remember Grandpa Adams doing this," she said; "getting me into a snowsuit and making sure that everything was tight and snug, my mittens clipped firmly to my cuffs and all, then, when I came inside all wet he unzipped me. He was very careful and always said 'Lift

[94]

your chinny-chin-chin' so my skin wouldn't get pinched."
I hung the parka on a bedpost. "Now the sweater..." She
raised her arms above her head and I lifted off the
sweater. "The blouse..." She had to help me with the
buttons my hands were so numb, half from nervousness,
half from the cold. "The skirt..." I unbuttoned, I unzipped—it fell to the floor. "You may have a little trouble
with the bra, but I refuse to help..." I at first tried it the
professional way, reaching around behind her to unfasten
the clasp. She stood very still, her arms at her sides, and
occasionally kissed me on the cheek. Then she began to
giggle when I couldn't get it unhooked, and I began to
giggle, too. I wound up going around behind her and almost picking the damn thing apart. She was very patient.
Much more patient than I would have been threatened
with freezing to death. She took off her panties herself.
And there she was: in the raw except for her loafers and
glasses.

"This," she said, her eyes closed, turning around in a
stiff little circle like a wind-up toy, "is a female member of
homo sapiens. It is not a particularly healthy specimen
nor a particularly interesting one. It would probably look
better in the summertime, because right now it is freezing
to death..." and her teeth began to chatter violently.

She certainly was little without her clothes on. Her
breasts were very small; her arms skinny, very bony at
the elbows; her hips wider than they seemed clothed, and
the pelvic bones jutted out; and she had a funny little pot
beginning below her navel. Her skin was a very pale white
and the spots of acne on her back below either shoulder
showed up purple in the cold, as did her lips. "I must
look," she said, "like death warmed over." And that she

did. "Not everybody is a Marilyn Monroe," she said. No, not everyone was. "I-I can't s-stand here much l-l-longer," she concluded.

"Okay," I said.

"Okay, what?"

"I don't know. Just ... just okay. I like—I love—you ..."

"You're not going to throw me out into the snow?"

"No ... of course not. What do you mean?" I kissed her very self-consciously on the forehead.

"Then Brother," she said happily, "I am going to bomb that pad!"

Two seconds it took her to scramble into the sack. She drew the sheets, blankets, and spread tight about her chin, and soon some color drained back into her face.

"Okay, Rudolph Valentino," she said smugly; "your turn."

I stripped down quickly and presented myself for inspection and Holy Shit, but was it ever cold in there!

"Are you going to make a speech or are you just going to stand out there pretending to be a machine gun?" she asked, referring to my teeth.

I began to fumble frantically in my coat pockets for the rubbers, and when Pookie asked me what I was looking for, I answered "the things." She asked me what I meant; rubbers? safes? skins? prophylactics? contraceptives? I nodded wretchedly and she said never mind. I said the hell you say never mind, I'm stupid but not that stupid, and she said okay, then if she got pregnant she wouldn't even call me up, I wouldn't have to marry her, nothing. She said she could count days and what's more feel and keep track of what went on inside her and she should know when it was safe and when it wasn't safe for her to do what we were about to do.

"Now," she said, "you better get in the pad because your sword is turning blue." She added; "You certainly do have a popped bellybutton. I've never seen one so extended; is it all right?"

Damned if—crawling between frozen sheets on my side of the bed—I would answer that. We lay that way, far apart, for the longest time. At long last, as I was preparing to move closer to her, she said, "All right; who gets the lights? You? Or me?"

"Oh, mmmpfh."

"We'll throw for it then. Odds or evens?"

I picked odds. On three, we thrust our hands out from the sheets. I had one finger out, Pookie had one also which she immediately changed to two. I complained but she insisted that two had been what she had planned to throw from the start and the finger had gotten stuck. We settled on a rerun. "I'm going to throw two again just to be fair," she said. I thought she was saying that to make me throw out one finger again, and then I thought she wanted me to think that way to get me to throw out two against the one she was going to throw, so I threw two—our combined total was three.

"Nobody outthinks an Adams," she said as, shivering, I quickly switched off the lights.

We lay in absolute silence in the darkness. The wind was blowing very hard, driving flakes of snow against our cabin. The flakes seemed to be popping. And the cabin seemed to be swaying a little, first to one side, then to the other. I began to feel seasick. I was sweating like the devil, yet freezing cold. There were so many noises out-

[97]

side 1 could only distinguish the silence close around us.

Pookie whispered; "Groan. Uneasy shifting. Silence. Heartbeats ... Jerry, remember how we were going to be so grownup about this? Remember what you promised me in your letter? A bed instead of the back seat of a car or a field, and all that?"

"Rome wasn't built in a day ..."

"That may be true, but I can be made in five minutes." She took my hand. "Now relax, for God's sake. We'll hold hands and get used to each other some more. It's not as if we'd never been in a bed before, you know. It's not as if we never made out, honey ..."

So we held hands and inched closer to each other, and pretty soon we were as side by side as side can be. Pookie began to talk, in a singsong whisper that got louder as she went along; but at first I could hardly hear. Boiled down, it went something like this:

"Maresidoesidoesidoesanliddleambsidivy: liddlekidleativytoo ... early one morning in the middle of the night, two dead boys got up to fight; back to back they faced each other, drew their swords and shot one another, and speaking of swords, I know I am getting a rise out of you, Jerry, look deep, deep, deeper into my eyes ..."

I had to kiss her to shut her up. One kiss led to another, and just before things got really rolling, she said, "Jerry, if any of your God damn scientist friends dump us into boiling water in the middle of this ...!" She'd forgotten to take off her glasses so I removed them for her and put them under her pillow ...

Later, before going to sleep, we lay on our backs letting the experience drain slowly and regretfully from us.

Pookie put her hand on my stomach, fingertips puttering absent-mindedly up and down.

"I can feel them," she said quietly.

"Feel what?"

"The bubbles in there."

I listened and sure enough; I could just barely hear something going on down below.

"A necklace of bubbles," Pookie said; "they're tickling my hand."

"It must have been something I raped," I replied languidly.

She giggled fleetingly and then turned very serious: her thumb rubbed over my navel, slowly, as if trying to erase a small stain.

"Jerry," she whispered, "do you think that maybe just one of those little spermata-whateveryoucallems might, in spite of circumstances to the contrary, make it home?"

"Pookie," I said, a bit alarmed; "you told me before we—"

"I know. But doesn't it make you feel sad to kill a billion potential kids in one lickety-split shot?"

"Nope."

"But think of all those frantic tadpole guys trying like blue blazes to climb up my insides, and all of them dying, one after another, shrivelling up and getting washed right back down and out to sea."

"It's a tough life..."

"Don't you ever think about how you too were once the size of about one fiftieth of a comma yourself? Don't you even want one of them to be successful? Have you no feeling for the underdog?"

"None whatsoever."

After a minute, she said, "Are you going to sleep?"

"Mmm..."

She put her lips to my ear and blew softly.

"I'm a wind, Jerry. I'm going to blow you away..."

"Mmm..."

Just before I went to sleep, she asked, "How many?"

"How many what?"

"Stomachs..."

"Eleven?"

"Yup..."

I must still have been smiling when I went to sleep.

I awoke the next morning alone in bed. Pookie, dressed in my overcoat and her loafers, was at the window, outlined in sunlight.

"Come and see," she said very quietly, her breath frosting the pane. "The sun is shining, and everywhere there are drifts of powdered gold as high as mountains."

I went; and there were.

CHAPTER FIVE

W<small>HY</small> I didn't flunk out of school between Winter
Carnival and spring vacation of my sophomore year I'll
never know. Because as a scholar during that time, I was
dead. As a lover, however, I had just been born: my
heart bloomed into a most rare and irrational flower.

Guessing conservatively, I must have married Pookie
at least a million times every week. Married her and
driven off with crepe streamers smoking behind us and
tin cans thundering as she combed the rice kernels from
my hair, and I with my free hand brushed rose petals off
her shoulders. Any given second—in a classroom, eating a
meal, or on the can—I could suddenly become mature and
distinguished: a responsible man with a car, Blue Cross,
and life insurance; bassinets, baby carriages, a house—
"Settling down." Boy, was it ever going to be great to
settle down and have a kid: my kid, Jerry Payne Jr. Hand-
somest kid on the block. Quietest kid on the block. Smart-
est little bastard you ever did see, and he wouldn't be
spoiled like other peoples' brats.

But the act of making this kid—i.e., grassroots sex—
was the number one diversion of this time. I bought all the
noted authorities and read up on how to transport both

myself and Pookie to fifteenth heaven every time we found ourselves in a juxtaposition. On paper I became one of the fiercest, most arrogant, most romantic lovers the world had ever seen, a tiger with incredible techniques, a Samson of enormous strength and unbelieveable staying power. Unfortunately, off paper—that is, when we were face to face—I was always plain old Jerry Payne who would not have dared suggest a preplanned souped-up coition for the life of me.

And the face to face business is what eventually nearly did me in: because by Thursday of every week I was so wrought up with the amorous heebie-jeebies that there was nothing to do but cut all of Friday's and Saturday's and sometimes Monday's classes and head for Pookie, which I readily did, much to the consternation of my professors. Then, to top things off, I soon became a pauper, having pawned about everything I owned for money to finance these junkets and buy Pookie little gifts. My father was very understanding when I asked him to supplement my allowance: he graciously refused, told me to find a job if I needed extra dough, and not to get the girl pregnant unless I intended to marry her. Very well: I took a Monday-Tuesday-Wednesday job washing dishes at the fraternity house, I earned my money, and to love I went. Needless to say, Pookie's alarm clock had quite a workout.

I woke up with a start several days before spring vacation, my head literally on the block. I had flunked three hour exams in a row, plus God knows how many quizzes, and I had term papers due in philosophy and English. Drinking and rolling, I moaned to myself in the cold light of dawn, had never exacted such a toll. There being only one thing to do, I did it: I begged for a stay of execution, promising to remain at school over spring vacation and complete the papers while investing myself with an entirely new attitude toward my studies, and, unable to deny my sincerity, the powers that be granted me another chance.

One thing was left for me to iron out: call Pookie and tell her the invitation to spend spring vacation at my home in Riverdale was off. With a palpitating heart and deep misgivings, I called and broke the news to her.

"You can't say you didn't have it coming," she said sadly.

"No, I guess not..."

"I guess that means I'll have to come up there, then—right?"

"Are you kidding? Pooks; I have to study. Work. Grind. I can't afford to mess around."

"So you'll study," she assured me. "I can amuse myself just fine. I'm the original self-amuser, remember? Poltergeists, banshees, flibbertigibbets...?"

"Pookie, if you come up here you know just as well as I do what will happen."

"No, I don't, Darling," she cooed: "What will happen?"

"I sure as hell won't set any records for getting work done, that's what will happen. We'll spend twenty-four hours a day in the rack."

"Jerry, don't be dramatic. What do you think I am, a machine? Nobody can spend twenty-four hours between the sheets: it's not healthy. And besides, the old menstrosity is due about the middle of that week..."

"The answer is no."

"Jerry, I promise I won't bother you; you'll see."

"The answer is still no."

"But Jerry, look at the set-up a minute, will you? Ten days with a fraternity house all to ourselves. How often does something like that get served up on a silver platter?"

"Pookie; I don't care what you think, or say, or do, I'm going to stick to my guns."

"You'll be sorry," she warned. "That first night you're going to get into your cold little bed..."

"I'll have Poopsick," I said.

"Poopsick-Schmoopsick! You won't have me! How can you bear the thought of ten days all alone in a big house with forty-five beds without me, that's all I want to know!"

"It won't be easy..." I said truthfully.

"You're darn tootin' it won't be easy: it'll be pure hell on wheels, believe you me. Instead of studying you'll spend all day looking in the mirror and yelling 'Jerry Payne, you've got your head up the old wazoo!' that's what you'll do. You'll stagger out of the vacation stark raving mad only to find that I've eloped with an Arabian prince, and what in the bigluvulating name of Sam Hill do you want to drive yourself and myself to that for?"

"Who do you think you are—Helen of Troy?" I asked, slightly irked.

"Helen of Troy...Jerry...wow! Okay. Go ahead. What do I care? Go ahead and blow the goldenest opportunity we ever had, that's fine by me. Be serious. Be studious. I hope you and that unbelievably gauche hound have a ball!"

"Pookie—you don't understand."

"I understand; only too well!"

"Pooks..."

"Pooks. Pooks! Pooks this, Pooks that—Pooks!"

"Oh, hell: goodbye then."

"Wai—!" but I had hung up.

I slipped the rest of my change into my pocket and stepped out of the phonebooth, head reeling. Had I done the right thing? Or was it wrong—all wrong? If Pookie came, would I really be able to study, or—? Or what? Had I no will-power? I charged back into the booth and dialed her number.

"Hi-ho," she said brightly before I'd even had a chance to say hello; "don't tell me, Jerry; let me guess. You've changed your mind...?

"I hate you," I grumbled.

"I hate you too," she said happily; "when should I arrive?"

Drowning, but no longer regretfully, I told her when she should arrive. Then I emerged from the phonebooth, left the house, and walked into a warm cloud covering the earth that was spring.

"Spring," Pookie said several days later. "I can feel it; that certain undefinable twinge in the tip of my shining nose, no doubt about it."

We were alone; the day was warm and fresh; the campus was spongy underfoot; you could hear spring seeping into the earth. In road ditches the remaining fingers of snow and ice had melted through last autumn's leaves, and we knew for certain that winter was at long last over...

But there was work to do. I set up camp on a card table in one corner of the living room, while Pookie scav-

[105]

enged the house. I hadn't scribbled off half a page, when she showed up with a large carton of plunder: some books, and innumerable sex magazines, which she said ought to hold her for a while.

"Jerry," she interrupted me a few minutes later; "would you love me more if I had breasts that looked like inflated nose cones and were always falling out of whatever they were in?"

"No," I said, trying to remember the name of whoever it was that exploded away in *Bleak House*.

"I bet you'd like me better if I were one of those girls in the Cadillacs, wouldn't you?" she said.

"One of which girls in what Cadillacs?" Her train of thought constantly eluded me.

"The ones that sit far back behind the glass partition and gaze out at you with pale frosted eyes, very mute and other-worldly. They have almost white hair, and it is always pulled tight behind their ears, lying in wound coils on their heads, with careful wings fluttering deliberately out in places to give them the polished casual look."

"What does that have to do with inflated nose cones?" I asked.

"Nothing. I just wondered if you'd like me more if I was a Cadillac girl, that's all."

"I'm excruciatingly in love with you exactly as you are," I said.

"Ah; that's better. If you'd only said that in the beginning, I wouldn't have had to go through all the Cadillac stuff."

She went back to the sex magazines, whistling softly as she turned the pages. At the end of an hour or so, she broke a long silence. "I bet they're all kaponized," she said. "Kaponized, shot full of pneumatic harmones, and rented out to magazines." And with this she changed to books, read for a while, disappeared, reappeared with pencil and paper, and announced that she was going to write a poem. But instead, she began to yawn, and was soon curled up on the couch fast asleep.

Sunlight through the large French windows colored her a rich gold. I relaxed for a moment to have a cigarette, and opened a window. Breezes came in smelling of damp grass and freshly turned earth. At the end of the cigarette I went back to work, writing in spurts, often stopping to wander off on idle daydreams. Poopsick appeared from somewhere and scratched on the front door. I let him in, fed him, and he curled up his angular form on the floor by Pookie's couch, his head resting forlornly on a bosomy centerfold, his ears flopped over his eyes, indeed a sad-sack of a hound.

It was amusing to see them dream: first Pookie would mumble something incoherent and smile, then Poopsick would quiver, lift his hind leg to bat the air a couple of times, and make a snufflish sneezing sound. I found myself laughing softly at their unconscious antics: I wouldn't have awakened them for the world.

Late in the afternoon when Pookie awoke, she suggested that it was warm enough to sleep outside. So while I scrawled away, she lugged mattresses out onto the back porch roof. That evening we were as excited at kids going to rough it in a back lawn tent. After a supper of hamburgers (we ate hamburgers all vacation, that's how good a cook she was), we showered together, spending almost an hour in the stall, washing each other's hair and soaping our bodies until they were foamy white, then we rubbed each other down so that our skins fairly tingled, brushed our teeth until the enamel began to wear thin, and finally, wrapped in blankets, we climbed out a window onto the porch.

"Good Lord, Pooks; how many do we need?" There were at least ten mattresses set in a line extending almost the entire length of the roof.

"I thought we might want to tumble," she said.

But not right away. It wasn't night yet, so we sat on the edge of the roof, watching dusk grow thick over the forlorn stock car in the back field. Lights went on far below in the valley, and Pookie said there must be a lot of frozen fireflies down there. Above, the new moon was as thin as the edge peeled off a dime. There were very few sounds around us.

Pookie hugged her blanket up under her chin and said; "Don't you feel like we're in a science fiction picture? Either we're the last two people in a city, who—because we were in a park with a lot of photosynthesizing trees— didn't die when the earth's oxygen went off for ten minutes, or else maybe some flying saucer is about to land, and it's just now hovering out of sight behind those trees making a silent eerie whining noise, virbrating space dust onto the ground where, in a minute, it will begin to sparkle and make things disappear?"

I didn't answer; I was feeling very calm and lazy; my eyes went out of focus atop a distant hill beyond the town.

Then: a rustle beside me; Pookie let the blanket drop off and stood up. The evening colored her skin a pale oysterish color; light played in her hair like a watery reflection on sand. She walked to the end of the roof and stood there, her gaze fixed on the ground. I shed my blanket and snuck up behind her, then without warning gripped her shoulders, but she failed to flinch. She turned around and we kissed, the heels of her feet not one inch from falling. It was a strange feeling to be naked with the night wrapped around us: to feel air against our shoulders, backs, buttocks, and calves: "It feels like menthol," Pookie said, tiptoeing back along the mattresses to the heavily blanketed ones at the other end of the roof that were ours. She knelt and did a slow somersault.

"Race you to the center," she cried, flipping herself again.

I dropped onto the nearest mattress, and began to somersault towards her. Why we weren't killed in the ensuing collision can be attributed to the fact that it was our rear ends and not our heads that smashed into each other. We sat for a moment rubbing the bases of our spines, having decided that this was definitely not a night for tumbling.

"Jerry?"

"Mmm?"

"Do you love me?"

"Sure."

She waited a long time, then she said; "I love you too," and in the next breath, "I bet I'm going to get a real rip-roaring case of poison ivy."

I certainly expected that. "Poison ivy?"

"Sure. Every spring; it never fails. Always about this time, too. It's in the air or something. I think I catch it because of what I did when I was very little."

What could I say except, "What did you do?"

"I took a poison ivy bath."

"Oh sure: just filled up the tub with ivy and hopped in I'll bet."

"I'm not kidding; I really did. It was another one of those things like eating worms. Joe Grubner or Jay Farrell or somebody challenged me when I said I didn't catch poison ivy, so to show them, I picked bushels of the stuff, and, when my mother wasn't looking, carted it into the house. I locked myself in the upstairs bathroom, drew a very hot bath, and mashed the leaves around in the water with the toilet plunger. Then I got in and really swabbed myself down..."

"I don't believe it..."

"But it's God's own truth. You should have seen the case I came up with. The only place I didn't have it was on my tongue! Ever since then, all I have to do is look at the stuff and my eyeballs begin to itch. It's crazy..."

"I guess so..."

A breath of cold air went by us, ruffling Pookie's skin with goose pimples. "The old cat's-paw," she said, briskly rubbing her upper arms and shoulders.

"I've got a better cure," I said, pushing her backwards.

"My skin is going to feel like sandpaper..." she warned, sliding her cool hands around to my shoulders.

We inched up on our lovemaking and slipped gently into it. The end was no climax that burst with a sudden hot rush, but rather a gradual spreading glow that filled my body with velvet and terminated eventually in a long slow climax during which we remained perfectly motionless, feeling perhaps that this consummation might last an eternity if only we were able to never move again.

When we both simultaneously awoke, it was still dark, but with a faint suggestion of light to the east. In the top of a bare linden tree some twenty yards away, two crows had landed. They saw us move, and like nightmares silently took off.

"Damn!" Pookie whispered.

"What's the matter?"

"I was having this dream ..."

"About what?"

"Well, I was stuffing spaghetti into my old white figure skates—don't ask me why—and off in a snowy corner Grandpa Adams was snipping out Casey Ruggles strips. I had a big pile of newspapers in front of me, and what I was doing was selecting the pages that had the strips on them and giving them to Grandpa Adams. But suddenly I looked up and he wasn't there. I tried to put my skates back on, though of course, they being full of spaghetti, I couldn't. So I had to go barefoot. I walked a long long ways wondering where Grandpa Adams had gone. After a while I came to a desert kind of land, covered by a low silvery mist no higher than my waist. I went through the mist and came to a corral-like structure and climbed onto the top rung. Below me in the corral I heard some large things breathing, but because of the mist I couldn't distinguish what they were. All of a sudden, across from me and also balanced on the top rung, was Grandpa Adams, smiling, with a big egg-yolk splotch on his tie and a pair of scissors held idly in his hand. I didn't have to say hello or anything: we nodded, and he took out a handkerchief and began to shine the scissors. The mist thinned out, and I could then see several smiling and murmuring soporific sentimental-looking monsters, a lot like hippopotamuses, colored very soft grey. I found that in my hand I had a lot of twigs, so from time to time, I broke

[111]

one off and threw it at the monsters' feet: they shuffled, momentarily frightened, and regarded me with their big beautiful sad eyes. Each time I threw a twig, I noticed that Grandpa Adams moved his lips, telling me something, but I couldn't hear a thing, so I started desperately trying to read his lips ..."

"Is that all?"

"Yes; then those damn crows came. I hate crows. I'm going to shoot one."

"What are you going to do—point your finger at them and say 'Bang'?"

" 'Course not. Yesterday I came across a load of guns in a closet."

She was right; there was quite a collection of .22's in the house manager's closet. The brothers used them to shoot at the stock car or at bottles and jars planted in the field or set atop the car. Most of this gunning originated from the back porch or its roof, and it was a principal method of whiling away lazy spring afternoons. Bagging a crow, however, turned out to be slightly more difficult than potting stock cars and bottles.

The first step in our vendetta was to go downtown and buy about ten boxes of high-powered shells. On our return, we carted several wooden cases of empty Coke bottles out from the boiler room and set up the bottles in a long line across the back field. We then retired to the porch roof, and, comfortably prone on our mattresses, we blasted away for several hours. The bottles stood up well under our barrage until Pookie got the hang of it, then she went right down the row exploding one target after another. I had to admit, when the last bottle had tinkled into oblivion, that she was pretty good. But good enough to get a crow?—only time could tell. I went back to work while she hunted up more bottles, and then, straight through to dusk I heard the popping of her gun, the shattering of glass.

Early that night we sacked out on the porch, guns by our sides, and as we had hoped we awoke early the next morning to find the same two crows sitting ghostily in the linden. Now the problem was: how were we going to stretch even a finger towards our rifles without alarming the crows?

Pookie made a gallant, though fruitless attempt. With painful slowness, she crept her hand out from under her blanket centimeters at a time. But the moment her finger touched the gun, the crows were off, lumbering across the field and out of reach.

"We're never going to get them from here," Pookie said, sighting along the dewy barrel of her gun at the tree.

"We'd better sleep inside," I suggested.

"Good idea." She put the gun down and scrabbled her finger over our dew-covered blanket. Even her hair glistened like strands of glass. In her eye there was a determined viperish gleam: reminiscent, no doubt, of her frog-skewering days.

The following night, after a day that had been punctuated by Poopsick's screams when Pookie gave him a shower, we slept inside, this time with an alarm clock to make sure we awoke. The window we planned to murder from was at the foot of the bed; our guns leaned ominously against the wall, loaded and ready for crow.

"This time," Pookie crooned, working me over with her lips, "we're not going to miss."

Promptly at four the next morning, the alarm rang.

[113]

Pookie punched it out and we were immediately wide awake and tensed for action. We rolled out of bed onto the floor and crept below sill-level to our stations, Pookie on one side of the window, I on the other. With infinite calm we raised our guns and poked the barrels around the edge of the window. But by the time our bloodthirsty faces dared peep at the tree, the crows were off and winging.

"If they can catch that little movement, we're never going to get one," I moaned. I was ready to throw in the towel.

But not Pookie. "I'm going to get one of those miserable black bastards if it's the last thing I do!" she swore. There was fire in her eyes.

"How are you going to do it this time?"

"Simple. Tomorrow morning we'll go out the front door and creep around the side of the house. They won't be expecting an attack from the flanks."

It sounded like a sensible idea to me. To make absolutely certain that when the crucial moment came she wouldn't bungle the job, Pookie again spent the afternoon sharpening her aim. At sunset the field shone as if it had rained diamonds, and the stock car looked more than ever as if it had been attacked by a flock of woodpeckers. We ate supper, showered, made love, and went to sleep with visions of big game dancing in our heads.

The next morning we looked through the closed window and saw that our two corvuses had once more alighted in their accustomed place. Tiptoeing with exaggerated delicacy, we snuck downstairs and out the front door. From there it took us nearly half an hour to creep around the southern side of the house, each of our steps being preplanned so as not to break a twig or make even a tiny noise. Nevertheless, when we aimed our guns at the tree, there was nothing up there but branches; bare, trembling branches.

Between clenched teeth, Pookie said; "I am going to wait up all night with my gun pointed at that tree, that's what I'm going to do!"

I tried to talk her out of it, but nothing doing. She had made up her mind to get a crow, and rest she would not until roast crow was steaming on our table.

The day passed slowly. I learned with sadness that the old menstrosity had arrived, and resigned myself to resting my aching loins. Most of our time—when I wasn't working on the damnable social comparison of Dickens and Carlisle—was spent talking and thinking about crows. We conjectured that if we shot one, we would then hold, among other things, the world's record for crows killed during a spring vacation at my school. In fact, we went downtown and bought a Brownie camera and two rolls of film to record the epic event for posterity. We ate our supper of hamburgers, I worked for several hours on my paper while Pookie read, then we watched the tube through the late movie which ended at three. Rubbing our eyes to clear them, we made a pot of stiff coffee and drank it. Then we went upstairs to take up our positions.

Collected pillows and cushions from various beds, couches, and chairs were arranged on the floor in such a way that we had a comfortable aim several inches above the sill. Through the open window we poked our guns, and silently we waited. Twenty-five yards away, the tree of death unfurled its black branches against the night.

An hour later we heard crows begin to call over the far line of trees below the field. Night lost its thickness, and in the grey pre-dawn it was difficult to see anything. Thus, the crows were in the tree before we knew it, folding their massive wings with care, and staring with glinty eyes directly at us, or so it seemed.

"Go ahead, Jerry," Pookie whispered. Then, before I could do a thing, she shot. One of the crows fell down through the tree flapping wildly, but just as Pookie shouted "Whoopee!" it seemed to find itself, came out of its dive, and began to fly—although obviously in great pain—across the field. The other crow by this time was long gone.

"Oh hell, thunder, and damnation!" Pookie yelled, frantically working the bolt of her gun in an attempt to eject a jammed cartridge.

Even as she shouted, a miracle occurred. The crow, having passed over the stock car, decided it could go no further, and it collapsed in mid-air, falling with a small thud we could actually hear onto the soft earth.

"*I got it!*" Pookie screamed, instantly delirious. "Come on! Don't forget the camera!"

I got up pretty fast, but she was way ahead of me. Down the stairs to the first floor we thundered, then down the steps to the kitchen, and out the back door we bolted. I nearly broke my wrist taking the slamming door from Pookie's exit full against it. Running about fifteen yards ahead of me, she was quite a sight, dressed only in one of my white shirts which was now jumping around her waist. She waved her gun as if in a banzai charge as she hit the field. Right then I realized with shock that her feet were bare, and I shouted, "Pookie, watch out for the glass!"

Too late. She yelped in pain, leaped and then collapsed, falling almost as had the crow.

"Jerry, it isn't *fair!*" she bleated a second later as I reached her writhing form.

Geysering out blood, a good-sized gash ran along her instep. After a few abortive attempts at stopping the blood with my shirt sleeve, I carted her piggy-back to the house. Inside, I filled up one of the two aluminum kitchen sinks with hot water, and sat her on the draining board with the foot in the water; water that reddened in no time flat. I lifted the foot out and wrapped it in a dish towel which itself was very gory in a matter of seconds.

"I think we better get a doctor," I said, panic crawling swiftly up my spine. What if she should bleed to death before my very eyes? She didn't look as if there were very much blood in her.

"No. I don't want a doctor! I refuse to have a doctor!"

"But you've got to get it looked at, and have a shot, don't you think?"

"I hate doctors. I hate doctors worse than crows!"

"Pookie, you're bleeding to death!"

She stuck out her tongue at me.

"Oh, lovely; what do you want me to do, Pooks? I don't know how to handle these things."

"All I know is if any doctor comes near me, I'll drill him clean through the head."

"Very funny. And in the meantime if you die?"

"They'll call me Pookie La Gimp in heaven."

"Well, Pookie La Gimp or not, I'm going to call a doctor," and I did. He was undeniably annoyed at being awakened from a sound sleep, but said he would come since it was an emergency. The wound slowed its bleeding, and I piggy-backed Pookie up to the living room, then brought some of her own clothes downstairs and helped her dress.

"Hey," she said, buttoning her blouse. "What's the croaker going to say?"

"How should I know what he's going to say? Stick you full of needles and say everything's all right, I hope."

"No; I mean about us living together in the fraternity house. Isn't it against school regulations or something?"

"Sure. But what does a doctor have to do with school regulations?"

"I don't know, but I think we ought to hold him hostage until I leave."

"That's a good idea. But maybe it would be better if we shot him after he bandages you up. We could hide his body under the seat of the stock car."

"Jerry, you're making fun of me ..."

"No-o-o ..."

The doctor, a bald squat man who looked like a dodo bird, turned out to be a very sympathetic guy and a good sport to boot. Whether he thought we were nuts or not never showed in his face: as we answered his questions, he remained impassive, for all the world as if every day he had a case where a young girl cut open her foot while running after a crow she had just shot at four-fifteen in the morning. He slapped a temporary dressing on the wound and said Pookie would need several stitches and a tetanus shot, neither of which he was prepared to give, having in his grogginess grabbed the wrong bag, so I piggy-backed her out to his car, and off we went. Dawn came up very overcast; as we reached the doctor's office, it began to drizzle.

A short time later, sutures and injections over with, the doctor lent a very pale Pookie a pair of crutches, and drove us back to the fraternity house. I invited him in for a cup of coffee, but he said no thanks, he was going back to bed, and the sooner the better. Before stepping into his car, he checked his watch and said, "If you're going to shoot any more of those birds, don't do it for another three hours." Rain came down in sheets as his car pulled out of the driveway.

"All right," said Pookie. "Let's take that picture."

"Pooks, are you crazy?"

"Jerry: we are going to take that picture. Now."

Who was I to argue? I still have the picture, or rather pictures, because we used up one roll of film out in the field that morning. None of them came out especially well, however, mainly because the day was as dark as it was, and also because drops of water were streaking the camera lens. But fuzzy or wet or underexposed, Pookie is always unmistakably there, her gun held at one side, the crow—a huge black bedraggled thing—held by the wingtip in her other hand, her hair plastered in wet rings against her forehead, her blouse drenched and almost transparent, her Bermuda shorts looking anything but gay, and her wrapped-up foot in one of my athletic socks resting against the crutches lying on the ground in front of her. The only words I remember her saying were, "I like to feel raindrops dribbling over my teeth." She said that, and her smile was as wide and ridiculous as a Chesire cat's.

It rained heavily all that day, and I became progressively grouchier as, having terminated the rough draft of my English paper, I switched to trying to figure out what the hell was going on in Kant's transcendental logic. Pookie sat around quiet and depressed, reading, drawing pictures, and generally feeling sorry for herself. Poopsick slept fitfully on the chilly fireplace hearth wishing there was a fire, no doubt. Every time he began to whine in his dreams I shouted at him or threw a pencil at him to wake him up. These times he looked at me reproachfully: Poopsick the unloved, Poopsick the unwanted, Poopsick the stoical sufferer. I worked well into the night long after Pookie had gone to bed.

Sometime before dawn the rain stopped. The earth steamed in a hazy sunlight and mist tarried well into the morning. Pookie turned seriously to writing poetry, and by the time we broke off for lunch, she had completed one of the nuttiest poems I've ever heard. Down in the kitchen, while I squashed hamburgers (which by now I hated with a passion) against the griddle with a spatula, Pookie, seated on a tall white stool, one elbow resting on the metal rim of the huge potato masher, read me her poem: or anyway, she tried.

"It's called 'The Lavendar Grella,'" she announced.

"The what?"

"'The Lavendar Grella.'" And without further looking up, she read the first three lines:

"The Lavendar Grella's
A mighty smart fella
That smells in some crackular ways..."

"Hold on, wait a minute, whoa!" I interrupted. "Pookie; what the hell's a Lavendar Grella, or whatever you call it?"

"Does it make any difference?" she asked.

"Of course it does."

"Okay. Then a Lavendar Grella is really a sort of left-handed monkey wrench with a purple cyst in its navel."

"All right; you win; I give up, I really do."

"Jerry, I was joking. Get it—hah, hah—joke?"

"I know; I give up. Really."

"I don't like the way you say 'I give up,' " she said, lowering the poem to her lap.

"What's wrong with it?"

"It sounds kind of snotty, I guess. I'm not sure why it irks me."

"Well; are you going to read your poem or what?"

"Wait just a darn second, here. Just who was it interrupted and wanted to know what was a Lavendar Grella or what?"

"Well, just who was it wrote something absurd like 'The Lavendar Grella' in the first place?"

"Listen, Jerry; I only wrote it for fun. Let's not get all excited, that would be infantile."

"Not much more infantile than a monkey wrench with a cyst, I'll wager." I meant the sentence to be taken lightly, but even I could hear that it came out flat.

"Then I won't read it," she grumbled. "I had no idea you were so bigoted."

There was a long silence broken only by grease spattering and the chuk of Pookie's knife as she sliced tomatoes and onions.

Then "Hey," she said softly, as I fitted the hamburgers into rolls; "it was a stupid poem anyway."

"No. It wasn't stupid at all," I said. "I was a boob. I'd like to hear it."

"You were not a boob!" She slid off the stool and embraced me as I turned from the stove with a hamburger in either hand. "I'll read it to you right now," she said enthusiastically, her lips so close I could feel the form of her words against my mouth. "It's not very long, and I'm sure you'll think it's funny."

And she recited it, whispering into my ear, holding the paper up behind my shoulder, while the hamburgers dripped grease onto her bottom and cooled off. It went like so:

The Lavender Grella

The Lavendar Grella's
A mighty smart fella
That smells in some crackular ways;
Of pithafix potter,
Two danfield trotters,
And elegant corpulent rays.
There's a smacking of poodle,
A fleather k-boodle,
A boot and a shoe and a bike;
And sometimes quite nearly

The aftermath dearly—
Is leathery heathery tripe.

But cavalry riffle,
Nine seventy piffle,
And two times division of four;
Is sweetly silescent,
The fletterwog crescent
Of shallakaballister door:
The Purpleish pageant
Most cautiously rageant
Stove sinister Pie a la Stella;
When Fort Mitherford Blamber
Decidedly amber—
Captured the Lavendar Grella.

A timid-type dragon
Of lackluster pagan,
A turtleoid Androcloette;
A smokerish feature,
Bestialibus creature,
Is sparkling, starfull, you bet.
But radioheaven
Of seven-eleven,
His age short of twenty-five-ten;
A recounted ballot,
A croqueffle mallet—
Comes out fifty-twelve once again.

Now: no one has seen
The strange warfle-een,
Nor thought of a crew-cut puffownie;

[123]

And seemingly simple
Narthalogus dimple,
Is sightlessly half as much brownie.
But one thing is sure
Of essential allure,
In undobtedly nookerill cellar:
A shadow at first
May unquestionably burst—
INTO A LAVENDAR GRELLA!

"How about a hamburger?" I suggested.

"You didn't like it?"

"I loved it, Pooks; but how about a hamburger?"

"Jerry, honey; you know what your problem is?"

"I'm insensitive to absolutely hair-brained disjointed nonsense."

She munched thoughtfully on her hamburger for a moment, then said; "Don't you get any fun out of words?"

I admitted that sometimes I did, although what exactly did she mean by fun?

Before she could answer, however, Poopsick interrupted the discussion by entering the kitchen and casting his sodden eye at the griddle. He looked so sad we singed several hamburgers and put them in his bowl. The tip of his tail gave a slight tremor as he lowered his muzzle into the bowl, the closest he ever came to a wag. At least there was one member of that household who enjoyed ground beef!

The next day we cleaned up the living room, returned the soaked mattresses to their proper beds, threw all spent shells off the roof, cleaned the guns, washed our dishes, and scrubbed the living room rug on which Pookie's foot had bled.

"I don't like cleaning up," Pookie said. "Getting rid of all the traces is no fun." I suppose that was why she wanted scarlet footsteps to trace her progress all over the earth. "What am I going to have for a souvenir?" she asked me, wringing out a blood-mopping sponge into a muddy bucket.

"The Lavendar Grella?" I suggested.

"Oh, great..."

"I'll send you the pictures when they're developed," I added hopefully.

She dropped the sponge into the bucket and went out to the back porch. I followed her. We leaned against the railing looking across the field, past the trees, down into the valley.

"You know," she said, her voice almost sounding afraid; "I'd give a million dollars for it to be the first night again..."

Not a song stirred in our part of the world, and above us, hairlike whisps of colorless cloud blew frozenly back toward where the night had gone.

CHAPTER SIX

Spring vacation ended, and we parted, agreeing, for my good, not to see each other again until Spring Houseparty, a month or so hence.

During the following weeks I found to my surprise that my intestines no longer twitched every time Pookie floated into my daydreams. Not only that, but I discovered it was not overly difficult at attend biology lectures, thereby putting off Pookie's letters until ten. Thirdly, to suddenly find myself the owner of a free weekend gave me a refreshing thrill. Nothing to do but laze around, drink beer on the back porch roof, and soak up the bennies. My mind at ease, I soon vindicated myself to the academic powers that were: the next step in my forward progression was obviously to respond to the call of the tavern.

The day came: it was thickly warm and comfortable like the yolk of an egg. After a two o'clock class, I gathered together my laundry, and Roe and Schoons and I, our full white bags slung carelessly over our shoulders, headed down the long hill toward town. We walked gaily by girls in flowery dresses, men in shirt sleeves washing their cars, and old timers on stoops squinting and not really thinking about anything. We walked lightly by all this, entered the laundromat, distastefully stuffed our dirty togs into washing machines, danced out and briskly traversed the dusty street, bowed once to the Great Titanic Solar Disc, then entered the spiritual gloom of the V.T.

Predictably, Ronnie was delighted to see me back (God dammit all anyway; whatta ya say): he drew the first three rounds on the house to celebrate. With much animated talk, the debauch soon ground into high gear, and when we finally sputtered to a halt for lack of funds, the laundromat was closed; a clock on the wall over the dryers said eleven-ten ... twice. But so what? Staggering arm in arm up the road that led to the campus, I felt indeed like the Prodigal come home. What matter that I flashed and awoke the next morning thinking I had mistakenly laid my head on an anvil rather than a pillow all night? The cry of the tavern was a loving song, and pity on them that never heard it!

This is not to suggest I ignored Pookie either in thoughts or in letters—not at all. I loved her as much as ever: in fact, I was quite sure that I had progressed beyond infatuation—gone over the top, so to speak, and run expertly into warm, significant, mellow, lasting amour. I looked forward eagerly to Spring Houseparty; it was going to be by far the best roll ever, because I had my cake and I was going to eat it too.

The all new, stupendously complete (this time the Real Thing) Jerry Payne at last!

Friday afternoon of houseparties, The Real Thing, accompanied by his friend Roe Billins, took time out from a sour party to meet Pookie and Nancy Putnam, Roe's date, at the train station. Hissing loudly as it braked, the train slugged to a stop; Pookie jumped out of a cloud of steam, dropped her suitcase, and ran headlong into my arms. "You're a great big furry ferocious polar bear," she rasped in a sexy voice, voraciously attacking my lips.

Unsettled by the force of her charge, I lost my balance and fell over backwards: Pookie said afterwards that my head hitting the concrete platform sounded like a pumpkin dropped off the Empire State Building. For some reason, I didn't black out right away, and I remember Pookie's suddenly sad face inches above me, her lips whispering tautly:

"Jerry Payne, if you die, I'll kill you, I swear I will, I swear to God I will ..." and one of her tears made a hot spot on my nose.

Then people, roofbeams, metal columns, and train windows turned into a big pulsating negative and I fell into a whirlpool. I came out of the whirlpool a few minutes later, my feet clopping down the station steps like Howdy Doody with his strings cut. Roe supported me on the left; a bewhiskered man wearing a square blue cap held me up on the right.

"Am I bleeding?" I asked.

"He wants to know is he bleeding," Roe said, rolling his eyes up and away. "Tell him is he bleeding or not; make him happy."

Square cap, without a glance toward me, said, "Yep, Sonny—like a stuck pig."

"Head wounds always bleed," Pookie said, nervously forging ahead of us, holding her suitcase crosswise with both hands so her knees bumped against its side with every step. "Whether they're serious or not, they bleed like the holy blue blazes. I'll run ahead and get a cab."

She took the last two steps and began to run up a sloping hallway toward the doors to the main waiting room. She had gone no more than five steps when her suitcase snapped open, disgorging pajamas, wooly sweaters, a package of stockings, several tight balls of knee socks, some books, three tennis balls, a bottle of aspirins, a toothbrush and toothpaste, a pair of mittens, a bottle of perfume, a circular mirror with a wire stand, and my old friend the alarm clock whom I hated so much. I suppose it was inevitable that the alarm clock should start ringing; it was as loud as always and then some.

Our bloody entourage stopped. Pookie knelt quickly among the ruins and grabbed the clock.

"God damn bloody blastulated bell—shut up!" she ordered, fumbling with it as if it were a hot potato. But either the button was stuck, or she was flustered beyond coordination, because the clamor continued, hic-cupping occasionally when she shook it particularly hard. By this time several people had stopped to watch.

"Give me that blasted thing!" Roe said, deserting me. He took the clock and tinkered with the keys and knobs in its back. Then he tried to throttle it to death. At which time I began to laugh. I laughed so hard tears blurred my eyes. Somehow, while I was laughing, my hand must have gone up to the back of my head, because of a sudden there it was in front of me, dripping red, and an afternoon of whiskey sours threatened to leave my stomach by the upward route.

"The Goddam thing ought to run down," Pookie shouted, scooping her things back into the suitcase.

[129]

"What an alarming situation," someone in the crowd sniggered.

Then there was an explosion; little pieces of glass skittered away across the floor. Roe dusted his hands off, and for good measure kicked the clock—hard: it banged against the wall, ting'd once, and lay still. I must say I was tickled pink: if my head hadn't hurt so, I would have let out a cheer to end all cheers.

"Let's get the hell out of here," Roe said, ducking under my arm again.

"Wait a minute!" A porter stepped out of the crowd of bystanders. "You guys ain't gonna leave the clock there—just leave it lyin' there all busted an' all—are ya's?"

"What do you want us to do—" Roe replied; "give it a funeral?"

"Oh, let's just pick it up," Nancy whined, her voice very distraught. I'm sure she was on the verge of tears.

"You'd never know I was bleeding to death," I murmured, but nobody seemed to hear my plaintive cry.

"I've got it, I've got it, for Pete's sake!" Pookie stuffed it dramatically into her raincoat pocket and grabbed my arm.

We shuffled through the lobby, no doubt leaving a bloody trail behind us, and ran into problems once again with the taxi driver who didn't want "no bloody heads on his seat covers." So Pookie sacrificed her raincoat, almost smothered me with it, in fact. I let out a howl when the clock in the pocket started to crush its way into the side of my head, and she removed it. The drive to the hospital was not pleasant, as Pookie, despite repeated threats from Roe on what he would do to her if she didn't shut up, persisted in wanting to loudly know whether the taxi driver had had his heart amputated, or was it simply that in this cold climate it took hearts a long time to thaw out after winter?

"If I were a cabbie," she continued, "I wouldn't even let no stinkin' bum of a college kid wid a busted head near my seatcovers, not even if his head was wrapped in a hunnert pounds a mink, I wouldn't. Human life don't mean nuttin' next to a clean seat cover, I always says." She extricated a billfold from her purse and counted off a few dollar bills. "Do you think," she asked Roe, "that a fifty dollar tip is going to be sufficient?"

When Roe and Nancy (who was seated on Roe's lap) only stared at her, she disgruntedly stuffed the money back in her billfold. I could see her with one eye through a small tunnel in the material covering my head. She took my hand in both of hers, and, squeezing tightly, leaned over until her eye blocked out my peep hole.

"Picking up where we left off," she whispered. "I'm terribly sorry..."

I could think of no reply.

"How's everything in there?" she asked.

I nodded, whatever that meant.

"I wish I hadn't knocked you over," she said. "It's just that I wanted so badly to see you, know what I mean? We haven't seen each other in ages. I planned all week of how I would jump off the train exactly as I did and drop my suitcase exactly as I did and run and fling myself into your arms exactly as I did. You wouldn't believe it, but I spent hours, bushels of hours getting that 'great big furry ferocious polar bear' bit phrased just right: it's written all over the margins of my logic book." It

[131]

was then she told me that my head had sounded like a pumpkin dropped off the Empire State Building.

As it turned out, my head needed only seven stitches, but it took three hours to get them. Most of those hours were spent reading back issues of *Post* and *Family Circle* in the bleak waiting room after a cheesy nurse had decided I wasn't emergency material. On leaving the place after our ordeal, we were all dead sober and pretty grumpy. The taxi ride home was gloomy; it passed in complete silence. Once Roe mumbled that he sure was glad there was nothing worse than an "ill-fated roll," which, apparently, the weekend had started out to be.

This fact was confirmed when, arriving at the fraternity house and having paid off the cabbie, we made a bee-line down to the bar and once more ran smack-dab into disaster: somebody had blown the tap—the beer was nothing but foam.

"Oh, I sure am glad nothing's happening!" Roe screamed, and dragged Nancy off to another house. Pookie and I retired to the kitchen where we sat on high stools despondently downing peanut butter and mayonnaise sandwiches.

"A formidable beginning," I moaned. I remembered back to the sour party, basking in the early afternoon sunlight streaming through the living room windows. Who would have thought then that six hours later would find me stitched-up, bloody, and sober, in the kitchen (of all places), eating a sandwich (of all the things to do on a houseparty weekend)?

"Cheer up," Pookie said. "It could always have been worse."

"How could it possibly have been worse?"

"Well; we might still be at the hospital, or you might have been killed or something."

"I wish I'd been killed." My head was thudding like a heart.

Pookie circled behind me, and, sliding her arms around under mine, began to punch her lips softly against the back of my neck.

"Why don't we shack up in the tube room and make out all night long?" she suggested.

"In that flesh pit?" The idea had never appealed to me.

"What are we, super people that we can't mix with the commoners? We're some kind of fabulous fornicators, you with your golden penis, me with my diamond vagina?" Her lips fluttered against my ear lobe.

"There are places for that sort of thing, Pooks, and one of them doesn't happen to be the tube room. Besides, I don't feel like listening to all that grunting and groaning."

"Oh, pity. Do you find it bestial, distasteful, degradating? Does it offend the delicate balance of your refined senses?" Her hands began slowly to rub in circular patterns over my chest; her breathing was low and loud in my ears.

"Yes, I find it very distasteful. It's about as private as a Saturday afternoon football stadium."

"Nobody can see anybody," she said, her hands sensuously kneading my stomach just above the belt.

"But you can hear ..."

"You can hear. What can you hear? You don't know who you're hearing. Most people do the dirty deed alike. You're entirely anonymous."

"I told you—I don't want to." Her breath curled around my neck like a muffler.

[133]

"Pooks..."

"I'll go upstairs and get a blanket, all right Sweetie?"

"Pookie..."

"I'll be right back, Darling. You'll wait right here like a good little boy, won't you?"

"Do I have a choice?"

"No choice; whatever Pookie wants, Pookie gets."

It took her little more than thirty seconds: she returned with a bright green blanket. We sloshed through half an inch of beer covering the basement hall floor, passed the bar where a lone figure couched deep in a dark corner was singing a song about Hitler, who only had one ball, and pulled up in front of the tube room door.

"You better take a deep breath," I admonished her.

We opened the door and were hit with a wall of soggy heat. We closed the door and were enveloped in darkness.

"Hey!"

"I'm sorry. Awfully sorry. 'Scuse me."

"Jerry, where are you?"

"Over here."

"Where...oh, here. Give me your hand."

I gave it to her.

"Pooks: I can't see a thing."

"You haven't been eating enough carrots."

"Carrots, for God's sake!"

"Shhh; don't talk so loud. And don't worry about your eyes. You're not supposed to see a thing."

"What do you mean don't talk so loud? You wanted to come in here, not me."

"Okay, okay. Come over this way." She tugged on my hand.

"Pookie, it's stifling in here. It's nauseous."

"Why didn't we go to the Kozy-Kabins, then?"

"Because I wanted to have fun—socialize."

"We're socializing."

"It's nauseous."

"Bullguano. It's a slice of life. Something to tell the grandchildren. Now shh..." She stopped, and I could tell she was feeling around the floor with her foot.

"Here's a place, Jerry. We've even got a mattress."

"Goody for us."

"We'd better take off our clothes before we hit the blanket," Pookie said.

"Are you kidding?"

"Jerry: don't be a savage. I wouldn't dream of intercourse with my clothes on. It's repugnant."

"Repugnancy fits in just swell with the atmosphere of this hole."

"I'm sorry, but I refuse to have intercourse with my clothes on."

"All right, we'll leave, then. Go find Roe, or Schoons."

"No! Jerry, I don't want to leave," she whined.

"Then be quiet."

"Yes, sir; anything you say, sir; right away, sir."

We shuffled around on the mattress arranging the blanket. Perhaps a minute, perhaps even less time had gone by, when, trying to open my eyes, I found they were weighted shut. A loud electronic singing entered my brain, and, although I was aware that Pookie was loosening my belt, I could not respond. With words of love dangling from my lips, I passed solidly and gratefully out.

I woke up alone with the feeling that I had missed centuries and centuries of time. I felt my chin, and, discovering no long white beard there, looked around me. Dismayed spent blobs were strewn to the right and to the left, snoozing erratically. Faces seemed to have been battered out of a clammy clay; female hair frizzed off heads like coily explosions of grease; an odor as of the elephant cage at the zoo pervaded. Wasting no time, I found my shoes and gladly left the blobs to their rude awakenings.

Pookie I located easily enough: she was seated in the almost deserted dining room, a ten gallon milk can on the chair beside her, and she looked drunk. I sagged into a seat beside her and said, "Good morning."

"You crumped," she accused.

"I was tired."

"You crumped."

"Okay; I get the idea."

"Crumper!" She giggled.

"Okay! By the way; thanks a mint for sticking by me."

"What—I'm your nest egg or something? You have a chain around me? I'm socializing..."

"No, no, no." I smiled pleasantly. "What have you been doing?"

She explained she had gotten up at six and the first person she had met was a boy who'd been drinking all night, and they had started on a stumplifter hair of the dog together. Then the boy had gone off somewhere to pass, but before he went he had bequeathed her what was left of the stumplifters in the can. Stumplifters are one third vodka, one third gin, with collins added to taste.

"My shtump," she said, saluting me with her glass, "is thoroughly lifted."

"Any fool can see that."

"If we'd gone to the Kozy-Kabins, this wouldn't have happened," she said drearily.

"Kozy-Kabins. Forget about the Kozy-Kabins, will you? I'll catch up."

I went downstairs to see if I couldn't wrangle some tomato juice off the cook for bloody marys, but I had no luck, and when I returned, Pookie was gone.

Not far, though. In back of the house, planted around the sub, we had a tulip garden which bloomed traditionally every year on Spring Houseparty weekend, just so's it could be flattened. That's where I found Pookie, along with a few of the hard-core drinkers, stamping down the tulips. A townie waiter dressed in a toga of ketchup-covered aprons was trying to play "Tiptoe Through The Tulips" on a battered bugle. When Pookie saw me, she motioned for me to join her. I shook my head no, not being tuned I'd rather watch from the porch. She broke away for a minute and came to the porch wall. She looked up at me, her head level with my feet. Her hair was messy, on her cheek a large wet smudge of dirt gleamed, her blouse was unbuttoned almost to her navel.

"I'm getting the damndest kick out've catastrophizing those tulips," she said, poking the toe of my shoe which extended beyond the railing. "I fall up, I fall down, I roll in the mud, I'm brown and dirty as a four letter word, don't you think? I'm going to win the Oobas cup..." The Oobas cup was an oversized wine bottle awarded annually to the best tulip trampler.

"You're a mess, Pooks."

"I like being a mess. Come on down and be a mess with me." She twirled, lost her balance, and fell down.

I climbed over the railing and dropped beside her.

[137]

"Get up, Pookie, will you for God's sake?"

"I don't wanna get up. I wanna be a mess."

I started to button her blouse, but she hit my hand away, almost angrily.

"You keep your big filthy clawing clodhopping atavistic hands off me, you grimy sludge, you!"

She sat up and with her numb fingers tried to button the blouse. Probably for the first time she noticed she really was dirty, and brushed at a large brown stain, making it worse.

"Oh, Jerry," she said, giving up in despair and allowing me to take over; "it's all going so wrong!"

I helped her up and led her back to the dining room. Several cans of tomato juice had miraculously appeared on the sideboard, so while Pookie gulped one black coffee after another, I, with great relish, after locating a bottle of vodka I had long ago hidden behind the Encyclopedia Britannica in the house library, commenced my hair of the dog.

Things got happy and blurry: before I knew it, it was after lunch, and ignoring Pookie who was clean and tragically sober as a judge, I went to sleep in the sun on the front lawn.

She woke me at four-thirty, and while I killed a frosty to get the loincloth feeling out of my mouth, she told me all about the track meet she had gone to. She remembered in particular the two-mile run, and one stubby ugly boy who couldn't run for beans and came in last.

"But if only you could have seen him on the far side of the track during his last lonely lap," she sighed, and described how all around had been the green of spring, blue of sky, white of clouds, and lazing on the infield, athletes, their red and white and blue track shoes looking like brilliant buttons on their feet, here a boy leaning on his javelin, posed, watching, there a bespectacled judge in Bermuda shorts, posed, watching, and far away near the gym a yellow dog complacently scratching and watching too. Nothing nervous or exciting about Stubby—but rather something familiar, you could tell it happened every weekend. "When the applause began for him, I wasn't sure whether to laugh for joy or cry for the same reason," she finished.

Poopsick came stiffly across the lawn, stared at us a minute, then curled up and flipped his ears over his eyes. Pookie scratched around his collar; he slid one ear off an eye and glared dourly at her.

"The world of the athlete sure is different from ours, isn't it?" she said.

"What do you mean?"

"Well; I guess you don't get drunk very much: your tongue never feels like it needs a shave."

"No. You just run around in circles all day and blow your lunch when you stop," I grumbled. "Drop dead of a heart attack when you're twenty-five. Great fun. No thanks."

"Athletes don't drop dead when they're twenty-five. The better their shape, the longer they live."

"Yeah; Joe Grubner's a real old man by now, isn't he?"

"Jerry ... you bastard ..."

"Oh no, they don't drop dead," I continued, warming to the argument; "they only lose their teeth, smash in their noses, bust their heads, arms, fingers, legs, backs,

[139]

even their balls. Maybe I should be a football player so somebody can monogram my face with his cleats.''

''I didn't say you had to be anything, God forbid! I only—''

''Or maybe I ought to be a hockey player so I could walk around with splinters in my teeth...''

''—mentioned that I thought—''

''...so's every time we kissed, you'd get slivers in your lips.''

''—it must be dif—... Since when have we done so much kissing lately?'' she concluded abruptly.

''Is it my fault if this stark raving mad maniac knocks me over onto a concrete train platform? Is it my fault if my head feels like whatever you called it—a pumpkin? I'm supposed to forget about the buffaloes stampeding through my brain? I suppose every time I go to a train station I should wear a crash helmet or an air mattress or a parachute or something?''

She stood up, flames leaping out of her eyes.

''God damn it, Jerry! All I wanted to do was try to communicate to you how good it felt to see the meet, that's all! But trying to communicate with you is like ... is like ... oh, bullguano to you! I'm going to change for that miserable cocktail party!'' and she ran toward the house.

''Well I had a good dream!'' I shouted after her. ''I had the best damn dream I ever had, and you missed it! Hah!''

Then for a minute I felt pretty stupid, listening to the echo of my words, wondering what in hell they had to do with the price of eggs in China. I threw my empty paper cup at Poopsick who took the blow without flinching.

The white sheath Pookie wore to the cocktail party went hand in hand with her initial coolness; she sipped away at a gin and tonic refusing to make small talk, while I proceeded to get well tuned. Yet towards dinnertime we drifted onto the back porch, where, amid shadowy couples and the romantic backdrop of the twinkling valley, we kissed as delicately as two butterflies, then smashed our glasses on the sub.

"What was your dream?" Pookie asked.

Sheepishly I told her I had forgotten. Taking my hand, she raised it to her lips and kissed my calloused fingertips. Then, clasping the hand against her heart, she nestled close to me, her cheek against mine, and that was the way we remained through the first two dinner calls. It seemed that against the palm of my hand I could feel the shape of her heart softly thumping away, like something trying unsuccessfully to unfold its wings in that cramped space and fly away.

After dinner we changed into Bermuda shorts and sweaters and went house-hopping. I queered the evening by getting involved in a canoe race and some speed drinking, with the result that Roe, Nancy, and Pookie had to carry me home and dump me on a couch. For the second day in a row I woke up to a new century, once more alone. Pookie had passed the entire night in the house library where she had read the minutes of the fraternity goat meetings from 1912 to 1934, at which date she had fallen asleep. The stumplifter boy, looking like a pellet regurgitated by an owl, woke her up at dawn; so she was again loaded as I shuffled into breakfast.

"I dreamt I was a widow," she said bitterly, tacking her teeth around the rim of her glass.

Rather than argue, I kissed the top of her head, her forehead, the tip of her nose, and one ear, then quickly consumed several eggs and three or four stumplifters. By the time Roe and Nancy wandered into the room, I was feeling greatly refreshed, and, on my inspiration, we mixed up a batch of Purple Jesuses in a gallon mayonnaise jar and went to the college graveyard to have a party. The biggest tomb, a wide flat marble slab, caught our eyes, and we settled down on it to do some serious drinking. We all wore makeshift crowns of wet lilacs which had just blossomed. It took us very little time to get thoroughly blotto.

I was sitting on the edge of the tomb; Pookie was stretched out on the grass at my feet. She closed her eyes and sort of whispered how it was a perfect day, better than yesterday, the kind of day that came once a spring, or every Saturday evening at the end of a love movie. Petals were blowing in the air; all around the grass was a deep green, soft and wavy as silk because it hadn't been cut yet. We were alone, shut off from the outside world by a tall hedge bordering the graveyard. Occasionally the strains of a rock and roll band floated as casually as a leaf over the top of the hedge.

"Today is a rolling in the grass day," Pookie said.

She set her drink down and stretched out, arms crossed against her chest, and rolled for about ten yards down a slight incline, coming to a face-up stop in a jumble of honeysuckle covering an old stone. Behind her she left a flat silver trail in the grass.

"A rolling in the grass day," Roe echoed; "can you beat that?" Gulping enormously, he polished off his drink, then fell to the ground and rolled, his arms and legs flopping like a palsied pinwheel. He landed with a loud "Uff!" against Pookie, also on his back, and lay still.

"My turn," said Nancy. Happily, she rolled herself down the silver trail. She had hardly come to a stop against Roe, than I bumped against her, and there we were: four drunks in a tight row; all our world was a limpid blue sky.

"Let's not move," Pookie said; "not ever."

We lay silently, not moving forever. I would have difficulty finding a more calm, more pleasant moment in my life. It must have been like being in heaven; for a moment we were all honestly awed, quiet, respectful.

"Nothing is more beautiful than sky," Pookie said.

"Nothing is more beautiful than clouds," Nancy said.

"Nothing is more beautiful than honeysuckle smell in the spring," I said.

"Nothing is more beautiful than four lit stooges in a graveyard spieling on about what nothings are more beautiful than what other nothings," Roe said.

Bathed in breezes and feeling each other's closeness, we thought on our words a while.

"If anybody interrupts this, I'll kill him," Pookie whispered.

"Nobody's going to," Roe said.

No; nobody was going to.

"I'm going to reach up and touch it," Nancy said.

It was a corny cliché, but we accepted it. Her hand appeared in the sky, small and white and limp, the index finger not at all straight, but not bent either; just weakly curved a little.

"Michelangelo," Pookie said.

"Let's just be quiet," Nancy pleaded.

So we were quiet; oh, so quiet. At first the magic was there, then it seeped out. Nothing physical changed, but the something invisible, the something of spirit, drained out, until suddenly it wasn't fun anymore; until suddenly we were like a bunch of kids who, promised a nickel each to keep their fat yaps closed for five minutes, desire more than anything, after thirty seconds have gone by, to talk, talk, talk, and, just like the children, we became nervous, tense, excited, each sensing that the other was weighing the value of breaking or not breaking the silence.

It was Roe who spoke first. "I wonder if that booze is getting lonely with nobody around to drink it?" he said.

"Shh," I said; "I think I hear it trying to tell us something."

"I can hear it too," said Pookie.

"What's it saying?" Nancy moved; I became extremely aware of her breast against my elbow.

"It's saying 'Help, help, come and drink me!' " Roe suggested.

We listened: my arm began to glow; my stomach felt soft.

"It's saying 'Drink me, drink me, I'm getting warm!' " Pookie said.

"I hear it crying purple tears," I added.

"Ladies and Gentlemen," declared Roe in a loud voice. "Do we dare let this poor orphaned jug of booze suffer so?"

"Nay! Nay!" rose from every throat.

"And what do the Ladies and Gentlemen suggest we do?"

"Attack it! Drink it! Swallow it!"

"What about the sky?" Pookie protested.

"Sky?—in your eye!" Roe replied.

We heaved to our feet and scrambled fervently up to the tomb.

"Wow!" Roe shook his head. "I had this awful fantasy that for a minute there I didn't have a glass in my hand."

"But it was nice," Pookie said.

"It was humble for a minute." This from Nancy.

"Ev-er-y-body up for humility!" Roe demanded, weaving figure eights across the grass in an attempt to stop himself. It took him a minute but he finally got hold of all his limbs, and staring at us, blinking big gobs of sunlight out of his eyes, continued: "I drink to Miss Adams, to Miss Putnam, to Horror-show Payne, and to Myself, and most of all, *to the humility that myself is!*"

He strode between us and leaped chaotically upon the tomb, his long legs almost refusing to quit the ground. Then he straightened, his tall frame shaking precariously, the contents of his glass slopping over his wrist, down his arm, and onto my plastered head now colored purple.

"Everybody up for hu-mil-i-ty," he sang, his voice getting hoarser by the second.

[145]

One by one we clambered onto the tomb, formed a squarish circle, and raised our glasses high.

"I'm humble!" Roe shouted.

We drank to that; then to Pookie's humility, Nancy's, and mine; then it was my turn.

"I'm humble!" I shouted.

And so it went, even through Nancy's turn. We finished drinking to Roe's humility for the fourth time, refilled our glasses, and lofted our voices into the Hitler, He Only Had One Ball song.

Then, as like the thundering of the gods above we were climactically chorousing *"GOE-BBELS, HAD NO BALLS AT ALL!"* an old man stepped into the hedge's entrance archway and stopped. Tall but stooped, with snowy hair and bow legs, he blinked at us through rimless glasses. Words froze at our lips: my heart deep-dived to my very toes. It was Poppy Cobb; in his hand he carried a bouquet of flowers—yellow and white flowers. I looked at him, his white hair, the glasses sending out slivers of light as his head slightly moved, the flowers, and for an interminable time I knew something was terribly wrong but could not for the life of me figure it out. We waited and he waited, stretching the moment —like a high-tossed ball prolonged at its apex—almost past its credible duration, and not until he turned slightly in the archway, did it hit me: we were standing on his wife's tomb. He turned, hesitated, his small eyes casting a puzzled backward glance that riffled sorrowfully over each one of us, and then, the flowers lowered limply to his side, he went away.

"Who was that?" Pookie asked, her voice a tense whisper.

Roe and I explained that Poppy was the oldest professor on campus, chairman of the English Department, and a capable poet.

"He wrote the poem we're stomping on," Roe said; "it's in one of his books."

Each of us in turn read the poem; it was very simple:

> Thou hast not gone
> So far from me;
> Thy memory rides always
> The horseman of my heart
> Into Eternity.

"Let's get out of here," Pookie mumbled.

Having quickly gathered our belongings, we tried to wipe all the grape juice off the slab. Somehow there were a few mauve stains that remained despite our best efforts. Glumly we returned to the fraternity house and joined in the Sunday morning milk punch and fun. "An ill-fated roll," Roe said; "boy, I sure can call 'em." I got to playing the electric guitar and forgot all about Pookie, who with Nancy had disappeared upstairs.

When Pookie reappeared, looking very subdued, she said she didn't want to eat, so while dinner was going on inside, we sat on the front stoop in the warm sun.

"I sure do feel great," she said dejectedly.

"Yeah...I know..." I tickled around the top of her collar, hoping somehow to make her cheerful.

"When he came into that graveyard it gave me the same feeling only worse that I used to have when at Uncle Bob's cocktail parties people laughed at his one real but terribly unknown movie star," she said. "If you could only see Uncle Bob's eyes when that happens you'd know what I mean."

"Yes ... I imagine I would ... "

Exaggerating his strange almost sideways way of walking, Poopsick came down the gravel drive. He stopped a few feet in front of us and stared balefully at our shoes as if he were ashamed of something. He looked as if he'd just spent a couple of hours in a washing machine. Pookie patted her knee and he slouched over, his eyes glued to the ground. She began to scratch behind his ears, then leaned forward and sniffed him.

"Phew! Get a load of that, will you? If you touched a match to him he wouldn't simply burn, he'd explode, poor dog."

Poopsick lifted his paw to be shaken: first Pookie, then I accommodated him.

"We butchered him," Pookie suddenly said when the handshaking was over. "His moment never got off its feet."

"It's not as if we planned to disrupt his day ... "

"Oh, hell—forget it ... Go away, dog."

Poopsick lifted his paw again.

"I said 'Go away', you dumb dog. Jerry, does this mangy flea-bitten monstrosity have to sit around looking like a God damn cadaver?"

I dragged Poopsick over to me and scratched his chest.

"I didn't mean to be brusque," Pookie said. "It's just that I'm sick of mess and smell. I've had all I can take for one weekend."

"I understand ... " A fly landed on my knee and I missed it.

"I wish I could be like Nancy," Pookie said in a small

voice. "Lucky, carefree Nancy; nothing seems to faze her..."

Our parting an hour or so later was almost formal. We kissed, then stood with our arms encircling one another, wondering what to say. The more the seconds ticked away, the less there seemed to be to say. Pookie stepped out of my arms and took the alarm clock from her bloody raincoat pocket.

"You still got that?" I stupidly affirmed.

"Yes; seems so." She pushed the minute hand around with her finger.

"What are you going to do with it?"

"I don't know—keep it for a souvenir, I guess. Enshrine it in the Adams-Payne Hall of Fame."

"Pooks, why'd you bring it with you in the first place?" I asked.

She looked at me and shrugged, then took off her glasses and bit one stem, blinking her eyes against the inflow of fuzziness. "I thought we might need it," she said.

CHAPTER SEVEN

June, July, August; early September ... We walked along the smooth lawns of Pookie's campus, past quiet buildings shrouded in the first warm afternoon of fall. In the gutters occasional piles of early leaves were burning: smoke hung in pungent bunches over the college. Lazy giant shadows snoozed in the austere entrances to academic buildings. After a while we settled ourselves on the library steps and Pookie closed her eyes to the sun.

I had not seen her since Spring Houseparties five months previous. We had written many long letters, but as she was working for her father and I for mine, we had had no chance to see each other over the long vacation. I found the summer had changed her considerably. With a healthy tan, and filled out a little more in places, she no longer looked like a Korean orphan. But her eyes weren't so bright any more; tired and unrelaxed, they bespoke a listless summer of drudgery. She wore a sweater that was sort of the color of the tree leaves—dusty green and turning; a soft, waning color.

"l'm going to roll-'em this year, Jerry," she proclaimed. "I'm going to have a ball; not going to worry about a thing."

"Pookie Adams not worrying about a thing will be the day," I said.

"No, I'm serious. I'm sick of the psychotic role. What's the point? Life isn't supposed to be a lot of buggy questions. You're supposed to enjoy it. So I'm going to enjoy it. I'm going to drink and fuck and have a good time. I'm not going to have one iota of worry. Shake on it?"

"I wish you wouldn't use that language," I said, not shaking on it.

"Oh great. Pookie Adams goes normal and Jerry Payne returns to Squaresville. Wow. I've always talked like that, Jerry."

"Well, there are times when it's acceptable, and times when it isn't. If you're angry or if we're drunk, then it's okay, but just to throw in a 'fuck' for the sake of a 'fuck' throws you all...all off...off balance," I finished lamely.

"Oh." There followed a long pause, then she took my hand and said gaily; "All right." She smiled the same color as her sweater—soft and waning.

"I don't mean to be priggish or anything..." I started to say.

"I understand," she interrupted. "A girl should stay within the bounds of her femininity until the right moments. That's natural."

"Yes." But somehow I felt that wasn't natural at all.

"When's Fall Houseparty?" she asked.

I gave her some date in October.

"I bet it's going to be the biggest whing-dingingest roll of 'em all," she said, hugging her knees.

"Why do you say that?"

[151]

"I'm in shape." She slapped her hand against her chest. "I've been training all summer long. I'm even a passable speed drinker now," she said proudly.

"Great..."

"My record's five seconds. And you should have seen my old man's face. Instead of smashing the beer bottle on the floor, I chucked it out the window. The window happened to be closed."

I was visited briefly with a vision of Pookie practicing in her empty room, sitting alone on the bed, opened bottles for speed drinking on the left hand side of a card table set before her, a shot glass for whale's tails on the other side of the table, a wastebasket nearby for vomit—on the cork bulletin board the faded fish picture Joe Grubner took, and on the window pane, raindrops full of the same miniscule world...

"What's Schoons' record?" she asked.

"I don't know."

"Of course you do: you must have told me about it a million times if you told me once. It was that night he and the fat boy—the slob from Grosse Point, you remember—the time they stopped up the freshman showers with the asbestos fireplace guards and caused the flood."

"Pooks, I couldn't care less how fast Schoons can chug-a-lug a beer."

"But you idolized him for it, remember? He even kept it down. Was it 3.1 seconds, or 3.0 seconds, or 2.9, or what?"

"Does it make any difference, Pooks? I mean, my gosh—who cares?"

"I care, that's who."

"Why do you care?"

[152]

"Oh: suddenly I have to give a bigluvulating reason for why I care about things? Why I care about clouds, why I care about bicycles, why I care about windows, why I care about booze? I don't know why I care. Why should I have to give a reason?"

"You don't have to. Nobody asked you to."

"You just asked me to."

"How's that?"

"Well did you or didn't you just—" but she bit her lip, closed her eyes, and shook her head. When she opened her eyes, they were calm, subdued. She smiled and shrugged. "Here we go again: Adams and Payne, off to the races. Look at 'em go!" She leaned over and kissed my lips.

"Anyway, I can't wait 'til Fall Houseparty," she murmured, drawing quickly back as I began to respond to the kiss. "I want to get laid in the most fabulous way ever."

"What do you consider the most fabulous way ever?"

"I'm not sure. I'd have to think about it some more. First off, though, we'd have to spend four or five hours in the house bar soaking up Corby's and Cokes. Then I guess we might try the phonebooth—the wooden one in the basement hallway. And I'd call up Rev. Thintle back in Merritt, that's what I'd do, and all the time I was getting it from you, I'd be asking him what he thought about premarital relations. You'd have to be very quiet, though. You couldn't blubber out all your frantic little directions, because he might get wise."

"I wish you'd drop the subject; shut up or something." I meant it one hundred per cent. She must have known exactly how I felt, because rather than protest she shrugged and said nothing for a few minutes.

[153]

"I just don't feel like talking that way right now," I explained, breaking the silence.

"I understand," she said, slipping her arm through mine. "Don't you love the smell of autumn?"

She wasn't kidding, however, when she informed me of her intention to roll. At six o'clock on Friday morning of Fall Houseparty, I felt lips plapping over my face, and desultorily half-opening an eye, there she was.

"Pookie," I groaned; "what the hell are you doing here at this time of day?" She was supposed to arrive late that afternoon.

"I couldn't wait, so I got on a bus," she said, and, yanking the pillow rudely out from under my head, she brought it down full force on my stomach. "Rise and shine, hit that wine, Boomaga!" she chortled.

"I must be having a fantasy," Roe mumbled gruffly from his bed across the room, pulling the covers over his head.

"Don't you know it's against the rules for dames to be above the first floor of a fraternity house before seven?" I griped. "I could get tossed out on my ear for less."

She whacked the pillow down again. "So get tossed out on your ear, Lummox—the party's begun!"

Indeed, the party had begun: that particular one ended when Pookie introduced fireplace hunkering as the new fall indoor sport. We sat in the living room cinders during the Sunday morning dance session drinking gin and juice and setting the new intercollegiate ash-hunkering record. "This place just soots me fine," said Pookie for the five hundredth time, and had I not been brightly lit myself, I would have hit her.

Over Homecoming weekend we discovered a new pas-
time—football at three A.M. on the varsity field. Nobody
but Pookie and I (and a baseball glove which served as
the ball) running across the luminescent stripes and tack-
ling each other before the silent moon-whitened stands.
I'm surprised we didn't kill each other. Towards four in
the morning, with the score 60-0 my favor, the game
deteriorated into a roughhouse: I crawled out of it with
a sprained thumb and a bloody lip, Pookie picked up a
gorgeous shiner.

Shortly thereafter, the first calm snow flurries heralded
winter, Christmas separated us, mid-year exams followed,
then came Winter Carnival which we began with one
humdinger of an argument that turned into a fist fight,
and ended with a semi-demented passion period half-
buried in a huge snowdrift near the chapel. "I d-dreamt
I was an eskimoess b-being ravaged by a p-p-polar bear,"
Pookie stuttered, her teeth chattering as we ran for
warmth.

Arguments ... arguments became as second nature to
us as teeth brushing. Seldom did we erupt into slambang
affairs like the above, however; more often we had quick
nervous spats full of childish cuts and sarcasm. It got so
that we were always off balance together: one second I
would love Pookie so much my intestines twinged, the
next second I would dislike her intensely and sincerely
wish that she would take herself and her wisecracks and
go far away. It seemed that gradually our love affair was
slipping out of our hands altogether, as if, while our
backs had been turned, the same thing had happened to
our romance as occurred that moment in the graveyard

when we were enrapturedly gazing at the sky—the magic had mysteriously drained out of it.

My visits to Pookie outside of party weekends became few and far between, and, in such times as found us together relatively sober, we weren't at all sure of how to treat each other. "My damn emotional hand is all thumbs," Pookie once whimpered, nestling her head under my chin...

Then Spring Houseparty arrived and I did something which should have blown the lid off the whole thing. It all happened at the Kozy-Kabins (once more), this time during a motel party. Things had changed some since the year and a half ago of our first visit.

There were about fifteen people, ten gallons of whiskey sours, a few beers, two live chickens, a whiffle ball and plastic bat, two fraternity flags, and a sign advertising Ice Cold Watermelon—20¢ stolen from Jack's All-Nite Highway Mart, all jammed into one of those little rooms. Pookie was wearing Roe's jacket with the purple rabbit on the back. Also, over her shorts she sported a pair of black lace panties with my name stitched on in red across the crotch—houseparty favor. And her outfit was conservative compared to some the people there.

I had even brought my electric guitar into the place, and I played four or five songs, then the fuse to the amp blew. But by then nobody cared. I spent a few minutes trying to fix it with a bobby pin—hopelessly, so I gave up, and joined everyone else in singing the In China They Do It For Chili song.

In the middle of this pornoral marathon, Schoons screamed, *"Nigger Pile-Up!"* Everyone hit the bed in one crazy heap of writhing screaming bodies. The pile-up

[156]

lasted about thirty seconds. Then the bed collapsed. On Schoons' fingers. Without the hockey gloves.

Nigger pile-up concluded, we set to work again on the sours, dirty jokes, a game of whiffle ball, a game of pluck the chicken, and trading dates. I don't remember who Pookie was traded to: I wound up with Nancy Putnam who was drunk out of her mind for the first time in her life, no doubt. She was none too coherent, and very hot to trot. She kissed me as if all her life she had waited for this moment, and she permitted my hand whatever liberties it chose to take. I began to feel bad about the whole thing, but before I could feel very guilty, people began to crump right and left, and the big let-down set in. Still nursing his hand, Schoons threw the keys to the Bitch at Pookie, shouting at her to evacuate the candy-assed dead and wounded back to fraternity house living rooms and dormitories. Pookie complied efficiently enough: of all the people there, for some reason she was the least drunk.

On her next to last trip only Nancy and I were left behind: Nancy curled up on the broken bed turning greener by the minute; me sitting on the tube which had landed on its face on the floor. Two half-plucked chickens locked in the can were clucking away. I remember Pookie standing in the doorway, asking Nancy how she felt.

"Like a million dollars; oh, Pookie . . . why do we do it?"

"Search me."

"Is it fun?"

"I don't know." She was jangling the car keys nervously. Then she dropped them, picked them up, and dropped them again. I had to laugh over that: she glared at me.

"You'll hurry back, won't you?" Nancy asked. "I can already feel my bed, warm and comfortable, drawing me down into sleep... Pookie, I'm going to sleep a thousand years... I wish those darn chickens would shush up."

"Maybe Joe Palooka here," indicating me, "will do his good deed for the day and tell them to guano-off or fly right, eh Joe? Now, if you people will excuse me, it's back to the Bitch and her cargo of five snoring Falstaffs. *Exeunt omnes.*" And she left us.

A few minutes passed, and, tired of sitting on the tube, I moved my aching carcass over onto the bed beside Nancy. Her eyes were closed, she looked asleep. I lay for a long time on my back studying the ceiling, wondering if it was fun. Then, I suppose to see if she were really asleep, I touched Nancy's shoulder. She rolled over to face me with a moan, and before I knew it we were in a pretty tight clinch—very tight, in fact. I followed the rules for a few minutes, working on her blouse, her bra, her breasts: but then things got out of hand. She was wearing one of those kilt affairs, making it little effort to strip off her panties, drop my own trousers to my knees, and swing on top of her into position.

Mistake number one—a big one! She suddenly became aware of what was going on and screamed, really screamed. Her body froze for a split second, then she hit me, cuffed me, bit me, kicked me, and pushed me onto the floor. Jumping over me, she ran blindly into the closed door like a bird or a moth against a window. She fell backwards onto me, screaming again at the contact, and scrambled hysterically away, recovered her feet, then banged into the wall beside the door, at the same time

[158]

managing to turn the handle. She fell once more down the three steps to the ground, got up quickly, and began running.

Instinctively—I was much too shocked to think—I hitched up my pants and took off after her. She headed straight through some pines for the road. Once there, seventy-five yards separated us, and as you already know, I'm no runner. The sun was just coming up, a beautiful day, and I couldn't have felt sicker to my stomach if I'd tried. I settled into a desperate plodding pace behind her, losing little, gaining little. I must have felt like Pookie's pudgy track man in the two-mile run.

Far ahead the black speck of a car came into sight and slowed down. Long before it reached Nancy and stopped, I had identified it both with fear and relief as the Screaming Bitch, and, as Nancy, her head hidden against Pookie's shoulder, was saying for the millionth time "He tried to rape me! He was going to take advantage of me! He was going to go all the way...!" I arrived at the Bitch's side. Pookie fusilladed me with her eyes and I hung my head. There was nothing to do but, leaning against the open door and puffing loudly, nod that it was true. What could I say? Laugh it off? Don't sweat the small stuff? I managed to mumble at long last that I was sorry.

"He wasn't going to use anything," Nancy sobbed, "I know he wasn't!" and she must have really been upset, for she next said, "I'll become pregnant and we'll have to get married and I don't want to marry him, Pookie..."

Pookie patted the back of Nancy's head and stared at me. Not with the fire-and-brimstone of a moment before, however; she looked bewildered now rather than angry. Nevertheless, she said very coldly:

"You stink."

I nodded.

"I mean really stink."

I nodded again.

"Like a God damn skunk." Her voice came out of a vacuum; emotionless.

"I got the message, Pooks ..." I began to tense. I had no right to anger, but she was provoking it. "If it'll make her," indicating Nancy, "feel any better about the pregnancy bit, why don't you tell her she doesn't have a blessed thing to worry about? Explain—you know?"

"All right; let's all three of us take a walk," Pookie said. "Leave the car right here and take a good long walk. We need it."

We walked for a ways, Nancy between us, her head hanging low, sniffling from time to time. Coming to an open field, we left the road and sat down in some long grass at the field's edge. Far below us mist was beginning to stir in the valley. We twisted damp strands of grass around our fingers and you could sort of feel us calming down, settling. At the downhill side of the field there was a line of trees like in back of the fraternity house, and over them crows were flying and caw-cawing, reminding me briefly of the mornings a year before when we had anxiously sought to kill the black birds and love had been beautiful. It sure was going to be beautiful after this, I thought. A real picture of heaven.

Pookie began to talk softly, about how the drops of water on every blade of grass were diamond bugs. She plucked a blade and with it between her thumbs, blew a

[160]

harsh note. Nancy tried it and after a couple of blades managed to blow out a raucous note, like the cawing of the crows. I played stupid, failing in my every attempt, hoping this would somehow atone for what I had done. Down in the valley church bells began to ring.

When it was good and dawn, when all the crows had gone and the mist had risen out of the valley, we went back to the Bitch. I drove, Pookie sat in the middle, Nancy was against the door. Nancy turned on the radio, the only thing that worked (sometimes) in that car, and sang along with a popular song. She came to a part where she didn't know the words, and suddenly bellowed "Shit!" as loud as she could, to my knowledge the first time she ever uttered the word. As we neared college she said in a funny meant-to-be-sophisticated accent; "Darlings, I just came within an inch of getting laid." It sounded unbalanced; you could tell she'd rarely used that expression before, probably had blanched whenever she had heard it used, in fact. Now she began laughing, then Pookie took it up, then I joined in. I for one was very relieved. We apologized all around, I was forgiven for being a brute, Nancy for being a temptress, and Pookie for leaving us together in the first place, and we had another go at some hysterical relief laughter.

Schoons, in typical almost indescribable condition— wet, filthy, clothes torn to shreds, missing a shoe—met us in the house driveway.

"What's with the retard on the unit?" he demanded, slapping his hand against the Bitch's front fender. "One of the retreads flip its atoms?"

I said we hadn't blown any tires, gave him the keys, and attempted to slip by him.

[161]

"Hey, Boomaga!" He grinned, dropped his teeth and worked them expertly back again. "Hey ... where you goin'? The hairy dog is howling ..."

But I wanted no part of him. Before I collapsed among the bodies, mattresses, and overturned chairs in the library, I had called my constant rolling companion of two and a half year's time a reeking bleeding a-hole. Good naturedly?—hell: very bitterly indeed.

That afternoon Pookie and I waited dejectedly for her ride into the station. To be once again in the Bitch. Against which she was leaning. It was about four o'clock, the campus was pretty quiet. Paper beer cups and smashed bottles were strewn about us: it looked, as usual, as if a bomb had been dropped on the place.

"I certainly do present an exquisite sight," Pookie said. "Me in my shaggy sweater smelling like an old man's whiskers, my hair dirty and stringy, my grumbling stomach an ash tray filled with cigarette butts, my head flashing all three slides from the Bufferin commercials on TV ... All morning and half the afternoon sacked out, and I didn't sleep a wink."

Seated on a white painted rock a few feet away, chucking gravel pellets from the driveway at her feet, I said nothing.

"Just like in the Friarsburg depot," Pookie muttered. Then she added seriously; "Jerry, this weekend something snapped. You know when?"

"I'll bite—when?"

"Do you have to start getting sarcastic ... please?"

"Okay; I meant it—when?"

"Right in the middle of that nigger pile-up. I was on

the bottom of it and there was some guy—I couldn't even see him—practically giving me the time, and I couldn't do anything about it because he was squashed onto me like the top slice of a sandwich. It made me think of how my fishing worms used to crawl into a big spaghettiish lump while they were trapped in the coffee cans I used to keep them in. I was being suffocated and manhandled and my nose began to bleed; it was all I could do to squizzle over to the edge of the bed and drop onto the floor. I crawled under the bed for safe-keeping, thought better of it, and evacuated about thirty seconds before the damn thing collapsed. I wasn't even aware of when the whatever it was snapped. But it did." She snapped her fingers softly, then stared at them as if they held the sheared cord or frayed wire or trembling rubber band or whatever it was that had snapped inside of her. "Jerry," she said; "you might not know it, but this year has been a real whizz-bang stinkeroo..."

"What's been so stinking about it?" All I needed was a big long sob session to really put me in good spirits.

"Everything," she replied. "Everything from the very start. Remember my attitude back that day we sat on the library steps—how I couldn't wait for Fall Houseparty, how I'd been practicing my boozing, and how I wanted to get the old thank-you ma'am in the phonebooth?"

"We never did try it in the phonebooth, did we?" I said, seeking to divert her from the spiel I could feel coming on. "I'll be darned; the old phone booth," I repeated, shaking my head.

"Maybe we should try it right now if that's all you're interested in. Or perhaps you'd prefer to try it with Nancy?"

That ticked me off: "It's not what I want, Pooks, and lay off the Nancy bit, all right? I said I was sorry, you forgave me, now it's over and done with. Make it easier for both of us and don't hold it over my head, okay?"

"Yes, Jerry; all right, Jerry; *oui*, Darling." I thought she was going to scream. Instead, she looked up at the sky and banged her palms several times against the Bitch's side. I felt some remorse and said feebly:

"Pooks, this is ridiculous; we don't make any sense."

"We never make any sense."

"I don't mean to act the way I do; say those things. But suddenly you aggravate me and I can't help it."

"Well, why do you have to sit over there on your little mountain making snide cracks while I'm trying to tell you something serious?" she asked. She quit her eyes from mine, turned sideways, and with her finger drew some round faces in the layer of dust on the Bitch's side window.

My remorse was overcome by fatigue. I told her I didn't know why I made snide cracks, I was tired, very tired, my bones ached, my head ached, I didn't feel like talking, getting involved. "If you don't like me, ignore me," I concluded.

"Ignore you . . .? There's a crocodile gnawing on my leg, and I'm supposed to ignore him?" Unmistakably, there were tears gathering in her voice. She drew a line through her faces, then another, then she smudged them all out. Seeing her lips tremble, I no longer felt belligerent. As she took her glasses off and set to chewing nervously on a stem, it seemed a big wave swept through me, cleaning out my gripes, my frustration. I got up and went over to her; she looked down and away.

"Pooks—you're not going to cry, are you?"

"Of course I'm going to cry. What the hell am I made out of—steel?"

I don't think she actually cried. But she rubbed her nose and came pretty close, and all I could do was take her hand and stare at our feet. After a while, with my finger I began to draw squiggly lines over her breasts. She squeezed my other hand and looked up, her face lighted up with the flush of a wan smile.

"Now; tell me about it," I said.

"About what?"

"I don't know. About what you were talking about. Or anything. I'll listen."

"Oh." She hooked her hands in my belt, and pushed her toes forward until they pressed against mine. "You promise we won't start bitching again?"

"I promise."

"On a stack of Bibles?"

"Sure."

"Well..." She rolled her lips in some funny little exercises, then wet them. "Oh...I don't know." She stopped, thinking.

In the ensuing silence, I ticker-tocked my fingertips back and forth on the Bitch's shiny roof. Pookie stretched her arms out, her fingers spread, and began to make sweeping motions over the roof. The stench of beer drifted like a rotten pollen on the breeze; if you'd inhaled it long enough it was probably strong enough to have made you drunk, or sick, or both. I wasn't looking forward to Monday's cleanup. Almost dozing off, I came to with a jerk, catching the tail-end of what Pookie was saying.

[165]

"...a great big bigluvulating artichoke; you've got to nibble through too many tasteless leaves to get to a heart that's too small anyway."

"Come again?"

"Life," she said.

"Oh, life; yes."

Her hand joined step with mine in a small parade atop the Bitch. Then she said, "You know; I don't think I'm going to return to school next fall. I think I've had it, kit and kaboodle. I want out. Jerry, this makes the fourth or fifth party hand-running that I've hardly seen you all weekend."

"It went kind of fast, didn't it?" I felt low; very susceptible. I added; "I'm sorry, Pooks; I don't know what happens."

"It's not just your fault."

"Well, it's both of ours . . . but . . . you know."

"Someday it'll be different." She caught my hand and pinioned it against the roof.

"Yeah, someday . . ."

We turned to each other and kissed, standing very still, our lips just touching, the way Pookie said she used to practice kissing mirrors. Pressing together bodily a bit, blood running slow, dreamy, we rubbed noses. "If you gave me a pencil right now, I couldn't write a word with it," she said; "couldn't even hold it. I feel the way you feel that first instant when you wake up in the morning, weak and happy, before you start to think, before the fur starts flying . . ."

Then I blurted, "Pooks, it's been all my fault, really. What do you say we each turn over a new leaf, cut out the goofing off, ease up on the drinking, the roll-'em atti-

[166]

tude, and start seeing each other more in between house-parties? Why don't we begin by going down to New York for a weekend all alone, not to my home, but all by ourselves in a hotel room..."

"That," she said, squeezing me tightly, "is what I've been waiting to hear!"

We had just enough time to make our date for the weekend prior to final exams; then Schoons came out of the house with his bedraggled date, followed by Roe, and Nancy, and another weary girl. They all looked as if they'd been through hell. Everyone kissed goodbye dully and tumbled into the Bitch. There wasn't room for all; I elected to remain behind.

"Hey, my shoe!" Pookie yelled, as Schoons started up his heap.

I found her loafer beside the rear tire and handed it to her through the open window. Then I blew her a final kiss as the Bitch peeled out of the driveway, pebbles flying.

CHAPTER EIGHT

Separate Friday morning trains took us down to the city where we met on prearranged schedule in the Roosevelt Bar. In order to escape the collegiate atmosphere of the Roosevelt and the Baltimore, we, or rather I, took a room (a single—in order to conserve our dough for more important spending—with a bath) uptown at the Henry Hudson just off Columbus Circle.

"I am bloated, I am jubilant," shouted Pookie, throwing herself on the bed. "Never before have I felt so relaxed, so free, so absolutely running horses and sunning turtles together! It's going to be a great big beautiful wonderful impossibly grand weekend!"

After lunch (cherrystone clams, frozen daiquiris, and eclairs) we went sightseeing in Central Park. It was a sunny windy day, a lot of white clouds in the sky. Pookie ran ahead on the winding paths singing snatches of songs. Her full skirt billowed around her thin legs, her hair blew crazily, she kept losing one or the other of her loafers. I put in more exercise chasing after her for an hour than I had had in the past two years all together, including intramural athletics and trips to and from the V.T.

Eventually she tired, and we lay down in the middle of a fairly deserted stretch of lawn. "I wonder," said Pookie, taking my hand, "if there does exist, even yet, a small blue cloud somewhere, and jumbled on top of it, or cocooned in the cottony center, are all the kites I cut free long ago. I'd like to think that someday I'm going to be walking along a road, or across a field, when suddenly all about me my old newspaper kites will fall to earth, quietly, without a sound, alighting as carefully as a flock of mute birds coming home early in the morning. And I'll read them: it would be funny, wouldn't it? Reading about old wars, and strange famous people: puzzling over clothing ads with curious limp hairdos, the men in double-breasted suits... And the comic strips: Casey Ruggles and...Well, maybe someday they'll all come home," she concluded abruptly.

"They'll all come home," I repeated lazily. Near us was a small rock with rivulets of crushed leaves trickling through its surface gullies; here was Pookie, a cloud bumping into her nose, a skyscraper delicately touching her chin with its spire. Blue and spring; couples everywhere on the lawns, stretched out in idyllic abandon; white papers fluffing about like Pookie's kites come home.

"I feel like a curtain," she said.

I scratched the back of her hand with a twig and allowed I felt exactly like a curtain also. And I did; I really did.

"I feel as if I were being billowed; as if I were empty," she crooned. "I feel mellifluous; I feel as if I were a dandelion seed."

Mellifluous. A dandelion seed. Will I have a dream some night—a dream with a black background, and will

Pookie Adams the dandelion seed turning in mute revolutions pass across my dream like chalk, leaving behind her twisty-turny trail that fades slowly into morning and disappears? With my twig I made a white x, a very faint white x, on the back of her hand.

"Well; so here we are," she said.

"Yes, here we are."

I nibbled on her cheeks and touched my lips to her eyelids. I kissed the tips of each breast and pressed my ear into the soft fabric over her heart; far away, like a sleepy drum, I could hear her heartbeat.

"Jerry...?"

"Mmm?"

"Do you like little kids?"

"Sure; I guess so."

"I mean, what do you think about when you see them?"

"I don't know. They're cute and everything, I suppose; I don't know."

"Don't you ever think that some day one of those kids will be your own?"

"God forbid."

"Why God forbid?"

"Getting up at two in the morning to feed the little bastard a bottle; shoving glop down his throat that he's only going to blow all over his crib five minutes later; listening to him howl all day long; rushing him to the hospital every time he swallows a bottle of codeine cough syrup; wiping him every time he takes a crap— that's why God forbid."

"Doesn't it impress you at all that here is a real live human being you made all by yourself?—you and your thing-a-ma-jig there? That maybe even looks like you, has your eyes, or your nose, or his voice sounds like yours, and if you want you can teach him to say 'Ontogeny recapitulates philogeny,' you can help to create him because he's yours—because the vanilla in him that's going to make him tasty or not is your soul?''

"Sure. And then he grows up. He shaves, he screws, he wracks up the family car, he runs away from home . . .''

"But he wouldn't, don't you see? Suppose we had a baby; we wouldn't bring him up to be an astronaut or a politician or a banker or something like that. We'd bring him up to be, say, a lepidopterist; something quiet and untense and pretty.''

A newspaper was blown across my legs: it came into view from behind the slight rise of Pookie's breast, and loped down the grass. A lepidopterist: what does a lepidopterist look like when it's born? Does it have a small gauzy net in its hand? Does it wear a white pith helmet? Does it have gaudy yellow wings?

"You've held a butterfly in your hand, haven't you, Jerry?''

"Sure. Millions of times.''

"I mean alive.''

"Naturally.''

"Holding it between your thumb and forefinger sort of at the base of its wings?''

"Uh-huh.''

"Then you've felt it pulse. It felt as if it were all heart, didn't it? As if in your hand you held a very small heart with very large wings?''

"I guess so; if you insist.''

"That's what kids are, Jerry—all heart. Big round blueberry hearts. The trouble is—the older you get, the more you grow away from your heart. Like a tree. It gets deeper and deeper inside you, more and more hidden.''

She raised one arm and flamenco'd her fingers. It struck me that I had no true idea of her mind, what it was like inside. I suppose I thought of something like spun glass or pink cotton candy, I don't know. I pressed my ear down harder, listening to the distant slow beat, the child heart.

"Until you grow up and forget what it was like," Pookie said. "But then, if you have a baby, you can see your heart again..."

"I know. I love you, Pooks. I love you big and wide and...I love you wide and deep and...I—" What the hell suddenly was the matter with me? To feel such deep absolute despair? To suddenly feel ice in my stomach? To suddenly wish I were far away? To suddenly want to jump up and run away; run away for good? I pressed my lips into her breast: her fingers slid tautly into my hair and pressed my head tighter against her.

"Imagine, honey, if we had been kids together..."

Oh sure. Curled up together, her hair lying in graceful sheaves over my fingers, her breath striking small flowery blows against my chin, her hands flat against my chest, fingertips pressing along my collarbones, her thin legs inter-tangled with mine... Oh sure. The Tadpole Pond, the evergreen tree, the kites... Oh sure. Eleven stomachs and sentimental monsters... I pressed my lips down, down, down almost through skin and bone, down to her far away heart, and she broke off speaking.

"Jerry, I..."

"Pooks; Pooks—" I was so surprised to see a wide wet circle on her blouse.

"Jerry, what's the matter?" Her voice was quick and nervous with apprenhension; she sensed it, she could feel it.

"Nothing. Nothing at all. I'm sorry. I don't know what happened." I kissed her lips, the tip of her nose; I smiled reassuringly. Her eyes were as large and wide awake as children listening to ghosts.

"I've done something wrong," she said. "What have I done wrong?"

"Don't be foolish. What could you do wrong?"

"What could I do wrong...? I know something just happened. It was what I was saying..."

"No, shh... I love you, Pooks. Really and truly, I mean it. I want to marry you. Someday we're going to get married, and we'll have a kid and bring him up to be a lepidopterist, what do you say to that? He'll look just like you and just like me..."

"Jerry: what did I say? For God's sake, what did I say that was so wrong?"

"Nothing, Pooks; forget it. I mean it, absolutely nothing at all. It's not a big thing. How about the kid, huh? What about the kid? Remember how you once told me that when you were pregnant you were going to eat all kinds of crap—hot dogs and onions, all that kind of stuff, so's he could hear bubbles in your stomach, set him to laughing? Well, we can do it this weekend, honest! And then we'll get married..."

Her body was rigid. I couldn't go any further, so I lay my head beside hers and wondered at the emotion that made me almost want to weep: compassion, pity, maybe love—I don't know for sure what it was.

"Jerry," she said very timidly; "do you think there

will ever be somebody—I mean like you say—inside of me, laughing and all?''

''Honest to God, Pooks. I'll put the little bugger there myself. You'll see...''

''You know: Aunt Marian and Uncle Bob—they almost had a baby once. Before it was born a very funny thing happened. Aunt Marian must have been eight, nine months pregnant, when, one day while she was holding a cup and saucer of tea against her stomach, the baby inside suddenly kicked the whole shootin' match out of her hand; the teacup actually broke, spraying the rug. It was a funny, joyous thing. Then, when the baby was born, it was born dead. And they never had another one. I don't know if it was simply because they couldn't, or because they were afraid, or what.''

Why of a sudden this stillborn kid? I sat up. The papers strewn around weren't kites anymore; they made the park seem dirty. The trees were a muddy color, gritty rather than fresh with spring. A short distance away a fat man lying on his back pushed up his shirt and caressed his vulgar stomach.

''I don't want to have a dead baby,'' Pookie said.

''You won't; I promise.''

''I'm probably full of God damn dead babies.''

''Pookie, let's change the subject, if you don't mind.''

''To what?''

''To—to anything.''

''Did you really mean what you said?''

''About what?''

''Oh; I thought so. You've forgotten already.''

''What have I forgotten?''

''About having a baby, getting married—that.''

[174]

"Yes. Of course I really meant it. Of course."

"Look at me."

I looked at her and repeated what I had said. She smiled, soft and waning.

"I won't say you're lying because I want to believe you, Jerry."

"I've been manufacturing lepidopterist sperm all day," I said, flicking a brown speck of leaf off her forehead. My voice sounded funny—sort of squeezed and untruthful—saying that. But she followed the lead.

"I wonder if it will be born all wrapped up in a silky cocoon?"

"Of course it will, what do you think?" I said cheerily, cleaning the hair from her forehead with a few swipes of my hand.

"And it'll have a hundred feet when it comes out of the cocoon, so I'll have to knit it that many booties. Good Lord, I don't even know how to knit!"

"Who cares? You can buy booties." The same cloud lumbered across each lens of her glasses.

"With a hundred legs we'll have one hell of a time clipping its toenails."

"Lepidopterists don't have toenails. Any fool knows that." My smile must have been very castor oil; but behind the glasses, I couldn't see her reaction to it: her eyes seemed transparent, half submerged as they were in reflected blue and white.

"What'll we call it?" she asked.

"Pookimum Jerriensis; what else?"

"Pookimum Jerriensis," she repeated, emphasizing each syllable. "A green and gold Pookimum Jerriensis with one hundred legs. It'll probably be a lousy dancer."

[175]

"Indubitably..."

We got up and wandered across the park, discussing our creation. It was not long before our talk died down: there was something sad between us as the sky purpled slightly, preparing for dusk.

"The stopper's out," Pookie said. "I wonder why the clouds, the birds, and that chip of moon don't settle slowly down to earth as the daylight drains away?"

She went on to chatter nervously about dusk and the rebirth of things that rooted and slithered in damp places: she even ran enthusiastically through the Macbeth witches' toil and trouble chant from the first poisonous toad to the cooler of baboon's blood. She was telling me a story about being chased through a grotto by white tarantulas, when we heard music beyond a hill, and coming round a bend in the path, found ourselves descending on a carrousel.

"Jerry, Jerry, Jerry," she cried, dancing ahead; "please take me for a ride on the merry-go-round."

"No; I'd rather not..."

That brought her up short: "How come?"

"Well...I don't feel like it, I guess."

"But it's fun!"

"Yeah. It's fun for kids."

"Oh." She clicked her heels and saluted me. "Yes sir, Mr. Grownup!"

"Go ahead if you want to; nobody's stopping you."

"Thank you, Mr. Grownup. I think I may just damn well do that."

She bought a ticket and left me alone to watch. She chose to ride, not on a horse, but in a gold-plumed chariot. The music started up, a giddy child's tune played on an organ, loud, and I suppose you would have to say happy, but desperately happy, almost frantic, as if the music in the shape of a ball were locked in a small room, banging against the ceiling, the walls, and the floor, trying to get out.

When the chariot came around the first time, I saw that there were some kids in it with Pookie: a pickaninny who resembled a baby unicorn what with a pink-ribboned pigtail standing straight up on her head, and several small blond children wearing blue berets. All the children were smiling; all of them had big blank spaces in their mouths where teeth were missing. Pookie was standing at the head of the chariot, facing forward away from the kids, her lips straight and unsmiling, her eyes hidden behind her glasses. She flashed by, and the happy toothless mouths flashed by and disappeared, and then they came around again, and one of the blond kids had moved up and was standing beside Pookie, who was looking down and saying something I'm sure the child couldn't understand because the music was so loud, and the next time around all the kids were clustered around Pookie, peering forward as if they were no longer on a merry-go-round, but off skimming over an ocean somewhere, drawn speedily by a team of strong sleek dolphin, and the painted plumes of gold adorning the sides of the chariot were real waves of gold, and Pookie, the next time around, for a short time the Queen of the children, smiled, and, as they swerved away from me into darkness, burst out laughing . . .

And was still laughing as she skipped back to me, pointed her finger at my head, and said, "Take that, you old kill-joy; I had fun!"

Fun. I smiled though I felt not at all like smiling. I felt almost as if I wanted to yell something at her but I couldn't think what to yell. We left the park, decided to take a horse-drawn hack ride, then changed our minds and put it off until tomorrow, settling for cocktails at the St. Moritz instead. We sat down at a sleek sidewalk table, and a waiter, frowning with sad austerity, said I needed a tie to sit there.

"If you bring him a drink he'll tie one on," Pookie said, grinning salaciously. I grabbed her hand and dragged her reluctantly away before she could launch into any of her conniptions reserved especially for unpleasant public servants. We returned to the hotel, flicked on the tube, and—putting off grass-roots until later that evening—spent an hour or so on the bed lazily fondling each other to soap and cigarette and automobile ads and the smooth voices of the five o'clock movie.

One thing about me you may have guessed is I'm a breast man. Which was all right with Pookie as she often said she had nerves traveling the straight and narrow from her nipples to her sex gland. However, I got—or rather, we got—carried somewhat away, and the next thing I knew she was complaining that I had wrecked her right nipple. "What have you been doing, Jerry; filing the stupid thing down with sandpaper?" she complained. She raised such a commotion, I was obliged to go downstairs for some Vaseline and bandaids. We fixed up the wound with a lot of giggling, showered together, dressed in our Sunday finest, and went to the Empire State Longchamps for dinner.

We dined on oysters, lobsters, clams again, and other richly assorted goodies; champagne washed it all down.

After Pookie had stored the last champagne cork in her purse (she'd heard somewhere that if she collected twenty-one corks she would get married), we agreed that we couldn't let our glow go to waste, so uptown to Trader Vic's we went. Impetus from the dinner champagne carried us through four Tiki Puka Pukas apiece—close to anyone's limit on this high potency rum drink—with the result that by the time we stumbled into the street supporting each other, we were more than pretty well looped—we were blind. My pockets were full of gardenias I had collected from the drinks. We made it around the corner for doughnuts and coffee, on the way serenading various New Yorkers with the In China They Do It For Chili song. I doubt it went over very big.

In the doughnut shop, Pookie damn near come to blows with the counter cleaner. The old dodge: she didn't want any doughnuts, just thirty holes, well wrapped, and she insisted. She employed a few four letter words loudly, and we were bodily propelled out the door.

"Screw 'em," she burbled; "let's go cross the street and break the violinist at the Plaza...!"

We began to cross the street and wound up in a dark perambulating thing falling all over each other, bouncing in and out of each other's arms. Every time we tried to kiss there was a sickening crunch as our teeth collided. By good luck, one of us remembered the Hotel Henry Hudson, and we arrived, were hosed out of the taxi, fell up to our room, and first Pookie, then myself, took a shower.

The showers helped but little. Pookie collapsed naked on the bed moaning about how she was going to be sick. I found the box of bandaids and began bandaiding her all over. I used up the entire box: on her neck, her breasts, her stomach, her thighs, her back, her rear end, her calves—the entire box, the big ones, the little ones, the round ones for corns. As I worked, I sang:

> I got bandaids,
> Jolly, jolly bandaids,
> I got bandaids
> To last me all my life!

and then:

> I got one for her left ear,
> And one for her neck,
> And one for her teeny little butt, poor butt ...

She protested a good deal but I paid no attention. When I was out of bandaids, I turned her over and began with the gardenias: "One for the right one, one for the left one, one for the belly button ... and one for the little pussy cried meow-meow-meow all the way home ..."

"Jerry," she moaned, "you're killing us both ..."

There followed thirty seconds of stark inactivity while the booze filtered out of my head and I figured out she was right. I removed the gardenias and fell beside her, futilely picking at a bandaid, probably the only right one.

She said, "Jerry, forget it 'til morning."

"I didn't mean it, Pooks."

"I know ... forget it 'til morning."

"I mean honestly ..."

"I know, of course, forget ..."

"I love you, Pooks; Boy Scout's honor ..." I even held up their three close-together fingers.

"Yes, I know you do, now let's get some sleep."

Misery, misery, misery: I think I damn near cried myself to sleep. I woke up twice during the night and was sick. The room smelled so overpoweringly of gardenias, I'm surprised we weren't smothered by the scent. Pookie lay on the bed covered with white shiny strips, breathing stertorously, and I could have sworn she was dying, she was so loud and yet so till. A strange vaporous blue light from the window gleamed in her hair and on her face as if a thin film of ice or a piece of tinted cellophane had blown against her head.

But dying or not, I was too sick to help her, that's for certain.

When I woke next morning, Pookie was in the bathroom. The door was locked, the shower running. From time to time I heard a retching noise, so I assumed she was, among other things, sick as a dog. I knocked on the door.

"You can go directly to hell, Jerry Payne!"

Her voice was choked in a funny way; so she was crying too.

"Hey, Pooks, what are you doing in there? Are you all right?"

"Am I all right, he asks?" She sounded hysterical. "Why don't you go fuck off, Noble Knight—you and your white charger!"

"Look, I don't get it ..."

"You don't get anything, do you? Idiot!"

"I said I was sorry, Pooks. I can't go on saying it forever, can I? Open the door, will you?"

"Sorry? Sorry! For the fifty millionth time in his life

he said he was sorry! Put that in your pipe, Adams, and smoke it!"

"Pookie, will you at least open the door so we can talk! Like people! What's eating your goat?"

"Oh, help, help, help, Mr. Noble Knight, a terrible cruel monstrous Gindergrudgit is eating my poor helpless little nanny goat!"

"Will you turn off that Goddam shower!"

"*What, so you can hear me? Can you hear me, Jerry? Can you hear my fucking feminine voice, Mr. Adult?*"

"You're gonna get the management in here in a minute!"

"Oh, now, wouldn't that be just too bad? Do they remove bandaids free of charge? Bolster egos? Patch up frazzled love affairs? *Let 'em come, then! Let the bas...*" She began to choke again. In fact, I once more thought sure she was going to die. It really sounded bad.

I pleaded with her; "Pookie, please..."

"Yeah, yeah; right away..." The shower gasped and went off, then the lock clicked. I opened the door and stepped into the steam-filled bathroom. Pookie had seated herself on the edge of the tub with the shower curtain draped down over her so that all I could see were her pigeon-toed feet. "Just leave me alone and don't look at me," she warned. "If you want to do something useful, throw out the gardenias in the sink."

I threw the gardenias out the window. Then I put down the toilet lid and sat on it. A breeze came through the open window and circulated through the steam, carrying out the gardenia smell. Pookie sobbed quietly for a while, and when she stopped, most of the steam was gone, a bit of the spring park was in the air.

"I feel as if my life had passed me by," Pookie said, her voice coming feebly from behind the plastic curtain. "Passed me by, tipped its hat politely, said 'Hello, Miss Adams, Goodbye, Miss Adams,' and once safely by, 'Screw you, Miss Adams.' God, how I wish I'd taken some moments of my life, Jerry—the good moments—and pinned their wings flat under strips of paper on cedar mounting boards to dry. Then, in moments like this, I might be able to look at their pretty preservedness, reach out and touch it even, just to know something good had existed, to have the proof ... but I don't have the proof ... Oh, pig manure, pigeon dung, bullguano, what's the use?"

"Let's get dressed and have breakfast and go on that buggy ride like we planned," I said. "It'll be very peaceful, I promise you."

"Peaceful, my fravenshaft! Peaceful doesn't exist anymore. Or I'm not peaceful, believe you me! You ought to listen in on the verbal hieroglyphics that bisect my mind sometime, then you'd see what all this peaceful baloney is about!"

"I can't see into your mind, though; I just can't do it, don't you see?"

"Let me paint you a picture, then: you're peering into this globish thing, see? There's a little figure perched on a tottering electric shock stool in the center. This figure looks suspiciously like me. It's got one horn on its head, half a halo draped around the horn, one wing, a barbed tail, one bird's foot, one cloven hoof. It's dressed joker fashion; one side white toga, other side red jacket and leggins. Above, hanging from the dome ceiling, are a lot of thin chords, at the end of each is tied a wooden handle.

[183]

The handles are labeled *R. Leg, L. Leg, Smile, Frown, Talk,* etc. All this suspiciously-like-me figure has to do is: receive electric impulses jolting up through the stool to its feet from time to time and react properly, meaning reach up and tug on the handle the impulse has demanded. Only it's drunk, this s-l-m figure, so it can't read the labels any longer. When it gets a *R. Leg* shock, it pulls on the *L. Arm* handle. When it gets a *Smile* shock, it hits the *Frown* handle. And every now and then, it tumbles off the stool and rolls around like a God damn bean in a helmet and nothing happens, get what I mean? A God damn bean in a helmet.''

I shrugged and said, ''Pookie, I don't understand you at all...''

''Well, why'd we have to do it?'' she whined. ''It could have been a perfectly dreamy weekend, and look what we did to it. We could have done any amount of touristy things last night: gone for a walk up and down Broadway after dinner, seen a play, had a bottle of wine and some foul-smelling limburger cheese in a little French restaurant after the show, or else have gone down to Greenwich Village... But look what we did instead...

''Today will be different,'' I promised.

''Oh, sure; I bet,'' she said glumly. Then, ''We sure do make a glorious pair, don't we? Agony in a Nutshell, that's us. Don't applaud, just throw wooden nickels.''

I said, ''Did you get all the bandaids off?''

Her voice thick with misery, she said, ''No; I haven't even begun...''

She drew the curtain back and I set to work on the bandaids, wincing at her yelps each time I ripped one off. It took twenty minutes or more to remove all of them.

Then Pookie lay on the bed and I massaged her back for a long time. She said very little the whole time, but she did manage to pull about thirty small white feathers out of a hole in the pillow. As I began to tire, she pulled the pillow over her head and humped herself into a semi-fetal position, stomach down, arms and head resting flat against the bed, rear end elevated Moslem-style. Her voice struggled out from beneath the pillow very muffled, very strange sounding, very remote.

"Here I am in the deep dark Limpopo Jungle where the Enchantment Weed and the Dream Grass grow, and stealthily over the spongy moss and Indian Vine and Spring Creepers steals the Prince of Love to catch me— the Moonchild who sleeps on a mattress of moonbeams and dew—to catch me in his great gilded net woven from the stems of Laughter and Chaos. Kiss me, Prince, and I shall evermore be thine. I'll get a job, I'll darn your socks, and everything will be normal. We'll even get married and have our toenailless lepidopterists..."

And then, of all the things she could have done, she chose the worst: she farted.

I was just plain disgusted with her and showed it by wordlessly leaving her, locking myself in the bathroom, and taking a good long shower to simmer down. When I came out she was dressed, sitting cross-legged on the bed with a piece of hotel stationery in one hand, a pencil in the other. Without looking up she began to read. Her voice was flat, emotionless.

Oh, Hi-ho in the Lavender Woods
A Sterile Cuckoo is crying;

[185]

Oh, Hi-ho in the Lavender Snow
A Sterile Cuckoo is dying.

Cuckoo! Cuckoo!
Cuckoo! Cuckoo!

In the real dark night of her soul it's always
three o'clock in the morning.

(F. S. Fitz—P. Adams)

"Is that all?" I asked, buckling my belt.

"That's all."

"What's it supposed to prove?"

"Prove—? Nothing." She crumpled up the piece of paper and threw it at me. "Nothing at all." She broke the pencil in two, and flipped the pieces toward the wastebasket beside the desk. Then she said, "Jerry, you may not know it, but I love you, I really do. I don't think I could live without you, and I don't seem to be doing a very good job with you..."

I heard myself say the same thing to her, and before I knew it, the whole bit about the suicide pact had come about.

Now: the confusion of the morning had put me at one of the lowest emotional ebbs of my career, and this may account for the fact that I agreed to go through with it. Or maybe the shower had been too hot and the steam had muddled my brain, or maybe with the king-sized hangover I had I figured I needed a lot of pills to knock it out, I don't know, but anyway—Pookie wrote out a one sentence suicide pact on another piece of stationery, to the effect that we were both doing this for love, and we signed in real blood, cutting our respective fingers with one of my razor blades. The method we hit upon (thanks to me) for ending our young lives was two bottles of fifty aspirin tablets apiece.

"We won't die with headaches," Pookie said, as I went out for the aspirins.

I entered the elevator sucking on my finger and wondering if below I should step calmly out into the sane world and walk away, or what?

CHAPTER NINE

T<small>EN</small> minutes later I returned with the aspirin bottles and lined them up on the desk. "Four jars of fifty each ought to do the trick" I said, beginning to wonder what kind of a fantasy had suggested that mutual suicide might be a good idea. I sat down in the desk chair, blew up the paper bag the aspirin had come in and popped it. Then I spent five minutes crumpling the bag into a tight wad and dropped it into the wastebasket. It made a loud ping against the tin bottom.

"Now what'll we do?" Pookie asked. "I mean; how'll we take them?" She was sitting Indian-style on the bed, chewing on a stem of her glasses. There was a scratch on her cheek that looked like the path of a thin tear.

"I don't know: take them, I guess. The regular way." I felt the way I used to feel on Sunday evenings after houseparties, when all the girls were gone, and from somewhere on campus a record player out on a porch was still blaring, trying to carry the weekend past its endurance point.

"You don't mean stuff them all in our mouths and then try and shove them down with a glass of water?" She put on her glasses and leaned forward.

"No, a few at a time. Two or three."

She took off her glasses, clicked the stems sharply shut, and leaned back. "It would take us the whole friggin' day just to swallow them." She shook her head and began to tear tufts of wool out of the blanket, and, after rolling each tuft into a ball, she set it in what soon became a row stretching from her one knee to the other. I said nothing in answer to that: for a minute the only sound in the room was a faint ripping noise when she plucked the wool.

Then she said, "Maybe it would be simpler if we jumped out the window."

That sure appealed to me. "For that matter, why don't we throw ourselves in front of a subway? It's even messier."

"Well, we can't seem to reach any decision about the bigluvulating aspirin." She reached behind her, grabbed the pillow, and, after yanking off the case, rolled it over in her lap like a mechanic with a tire until she found the hole. She pinched out a white feather, lifted it to her lips, and blew it into the air.

"How about melting them down in a glass of water, or something?"

"Go ahead, I don't care."

I got a glass of water from the bathroom, set it on the desk, and opened one of the aspirin bottles. I dropped a tablet into the water. It didn't do a thing for three seconds. Then it opened like a tiny mushroom cloud, sending little white chunks up to the surface. The rest of it crumbled outward on the bottom of the glass in a circular form, and settled. There was something very evil and unnatural about it; like the movie blooming of a flower in five seconds, or a miniature atomic explosion.

[189]

A feather went quite high, hung on the air, was caught in a draft, and planed downward into the bathroom. "They don't fizzle much, do they?" Pookie said.

"They're not Alka-Seltzers."

"Who said they were Alka-Seltzers? Who said anything about Alka-Seltzers? Did I say anything about Alka-Seltzers?"

"I was merely trying to explain to your thick head that aspirins aren't supposed to fizzle. Some pills fizzle and some pills don't."

"Like romances." She began to make feather designs on the spread. I dropped another pill into the water. It sank, waited, and then went into its crumbly explosion.

"You'd think they'd make a noise or something," Pookie said, not looking up from her feathergram. "I mean something besides that plup when you drop them in."

"Maybe you'd like it if they'd sing a song?"

"Maybe I would and maybe I wouldn't." She cocked her head, admiring her work, a large sun-looking thing.

"Maybe you'd like me to go back and exchange your bottles for singing pills?" I was beginning to hate her for her nonchalance.

"I don't care to answer that," she said huffily. She leaned over, her face only an inch or so above her feathery design, and blew hard. Feathers whirled in turmoil around her head. Then she straightened up quickly, another bright idea in her eyes. "I've got it, Jerry! What about that candy aspirin, the stuff for kids? You can just chew it up and swallow it because it tastes good."

I explained that we'd have to eat a crate of them because they weren't very strong.

"All right, then; how about a bottle of bourbon?"

"How about it?"

"Wouldn't it be less painful if we bought a bottle of bourbon and drank it before we took the aspirin?" There were several feathers clinging to her brow.

"A bottle of bourbon. That's just what we need."

"You don't have to be so huffy about it." She had her finger in the hole the feathers had been coming out of, and was wiggling it around, making the hole wider.

"Pookie; haven't we drunk enough for a while? I mean —if we've gotta go, can't we go quietly? Must we go retching to our doom?"

"But won't it hurt otherwise?" she asked.

"Taking aspirin hurt?"

"Well... what about cramps?"

"Pookie, you won't feel a thing, I promise you."

"Oh no you don't. I bet we'll get cramps, right in the old feed bag, and I'll bet it's pure agony. I'll bet we writhe all over the floor in agony. I'll bet we go screaming to our deaths."

"Let's forget the whole thing, then, for Christ's sake!"

"The whole what?"

"The whole suicide bit." I dropped another aspirin into the glass.

"Well, now, darn it, don't be in such a rush, Jerry." She pushed her finger along the blanket, making a line through the white square she had been constructing. "Why are you always in such a rush? Is there any hurry or anything? Does a minute here or a minute there make any difference in the long run?"

"No; no difference. Absolutely no difference. Absolutely no difference at all. Have a minute; have a year; have a century for all I care."

"You don't really care, do you?" She wasn't looking at me, but her finger had stopped tracing patterns through the feathers.

"About what don't I really care, Pookie?"

"About anything. You don't care what's going to happen to us, or me, or anybody, do you? You don't care if it hurts or if it doesn't hurt. You don't ... I bet you're going to let me swallow my shot first, aren't you?" she accused suddenly, looking up. "Sure; let me swallow it, then take a powder. That's what you're going to do."

I found it so hard to believe our conversation was actually taking place that for a minute I said nothing, completely stunned. Then a big bubble of fury exploded in my head.

"You are right, you are right! That is exactly what I am going to do! Blah!"

"I bet you hate me!"

"You bet. Oh boy are you ever right about that, girl; do I ever hate you, yes sirree. I never loved you or anything like that, oh no. All I've done is put up with your indescribable shit for two and a half years! No, I never loved you, that's why I'm so calm now, that's why I'm so God damn happy!"

"You put up with all *my* shit! I like that! Listen to God's little angel, Mister Jerry Payne, Boy Adult, shooting off his big fat blastulated mouth!"

"Oh, shut up. You bore me with your cute little expressions."

"I bore you? I hate you, Jerry Payne! I detest you!

I wish you were dead! Dead and with worms crawling ... oh, dammit! Dammit! Dammit!" Covering her face with her hands, she leaned over so that her elbows were tucked inside her knees.

"I'm sorry, Pooks ..." But I could think of nothing to say—I felt numb. And the strangest thing of all is, I wasn't numb with misery, or anger, or because our love affair was bolluxed up but good: it's just that something in me had momentarily shut off, and I didn't feel a thing. As if the moment before when I'd shouted at her had never existed.

"Oh yeah, you're sorry. Thanks for being sorry." Her words came to me out of shape, stretched as they were between the flats of her hands.

"I don't know what to say, Pookie."

She rubbed her eyes and stared at me. "Are you smiling?"

"Smiling?"

"I can't see you. The window's so bright."

"Oh." I snapped the plastic cover back on the aspirin bottle, and drank off the glass of water. Pookie rubbed her eyes some more, then, noticing a feather on her sweater, plucked it off. But when she blew, it remained stuck to her fingertip.

"Jerry; why can't I just take a bottle of those pills and die and go up to heaven and be an angel or something? Or why can't I stop being Pookie Adams and be normal, simple, sweet, polite, and happy? Why aren't there happiness stores where you can go in and buy three Happies for a nickel like that fruit juice that used to come in a wax tube and all you had to do was bite off the top and drain it? Or something, for God's sake?"

"Pookie—please shut up."

"Shut up ..." Her voice was very small, very weary. "Why must I always shut up?"

Was I supposed to have an answer? I said, "We never would have gone through with it."

"Jerry, I want to."

"No. You don't. If you really had wanted to, it probably never would have come up."

"I don't understand." Completing the fingernails on one hand, she switched to biting the others.

"I guess I don't either."

"So the game's been called? Rained out, huh?"

"Yes."

Pookie got up, and, after telling me to move out of the way, she very deliberately arranged the four aspirin bottles in a row on the window sill. Next, she opened the window and with her index finger jabbed each bottle off the ledge. For each one there was a long pause, then a flat small explosion. This done, she ripped the pact into confetti and threw it after the bottles. Then she closed the window, and behind its protection we watched the last of the pact flutter toward the sidewalk.

"We would have messed it up like everything else," I said. "Something would have gone wrong."

"I guess so."

She rubbed her cheek against my shoulder, and the coldness of a minute before left me. I confronted her, framing her face with my hands, smoothing the corners of her mouth with my thumbs. She tilted her head way backwards and a funny expression came over her face, a floating vague wineness filled her eyes, something more than tears, something that may have come from even deeper than her heart, from the hidden secret place, the soft magic incomprehensible center of her imagination, the lonely dreamy center of her imagination.

"Jerry," she began, her voice wet, forewarning tears; "why can't I just be a sort of taffeta debutante leisurely eating stars with a silver spoon? Or why can't I spend all my time sitting on a corral fence with Grandpa Adams, tossing twigs at big grey sentimental monsters, or be with him early in the morning having breakfast, knowing the fur was never going to fly? Oh, how I'd love to live in a New York world of silhouettes and top-hatted drivers and misty iridescent skylines, and I'd just as much like to live in a wet leafy world where brightly colored Glorious beetles fell off leaves into my hands every few minutes ..." Her voice cracked, and she bit at a chapped piece of skin on her lip. "Only ... the trouble is—those kinds of world's don't exist any more, do they, honey? Not even Nancy Putnam exists anymore; not the way she was anyway ..."

I drew her close, but she wouldn't nestle her head under my chin.

"Darling ..." she said, the word whispered, almost inaudible, and got no farther because tears came: like big clear pearls they welled out of the corners of her eyes and streaked around to her ears, leaving thin wet lines that might well have been shadows of her glasses' stems. She broke away from me and I turned back to the window, yet I saw no further than the pane: it was dusty, spotted with raindrop scars and several fingerprints which were like small galaxies in the glass. A few seconds passed, then a loud poumpfh! made me turn around.

She had flung the pillow against the ceiling, and it had

[195]

burst. With her back to me, stooped slightly, her body shaking all over, she was trying hard not to cry. Thousands of small feathers snowed down from the ceiling as from a slow wistful dream. They settled lightly into her hair; they landed slowly on her shoulders; they formed a white film over the television set; they nearly covered the bed, and the desk—and there were even a few feathers in the empty aspirin glass. *I love you, Pookie* seemed about to burst my heart; *I love you, Pookie* was in the tips of my fingers—fingers I longed to touch and soothe her with... But my lips were silent, and I could make no move. I could only watch helplessly as the last of the feathers fell and the room became very still...

"I'm so sick of crying..." she whimpered; "why do I have to do it all the time...?" and burst out anew.

We ate lunch at a drugstore on Ninth Avenue; hamburgers and Cokes. After lunch we went to the southeast corner of the park, but at the last moment decided what was the point of wasting all the money on a horse-drawn tour. We sat on a bench and watched dirty ducks swim around in the park pond instead. Later in the afternoon we went up to the zoo and walked around, leaving a trail of peanut shells behind us. From time to time we grunted to each other, that was the extent of our communication. Towards evening we drifted back across the park and over to the far West Side, to the river.

Standing on the edge of a pier parking lot, we stared down at thick grey slime littered with old tires, oil drums, shoes, springs, splintered wood, beer cans, and odds and ends of steel rods, you couldn't tell from what. Near shore, the stub ends of grey pilings, like broken teeth, pushed up. Brackish pools full of minnows dotted the ooze; elsewhere there were formless bumps where things had sunk out of sight, and occasionally, in odd places, bubbles came out of the muck. On the edge of this expanse, where the tide of inky water was washing back in, stood one ragged gull with no tailfeathers.

"It looks like one of those tarpit places dinosaurs used to fall into," said Pookie, taking my hand.

A strong wind blew dust in our eyes and rattled the dry stringy grass growing in the six inches between a wooden barrier and the start of the lot. To our right, beneath the overhead highway, empty truck trailers stood, their canvas tarpaulins flapping loudly in the wind. They were gathered haphazardly, surrounded by scatters of broken glass, small piles of crushed bricks, and puddles of green and oily water. Newspapers tumbled back and forth; there was no man nor woman beside ourselves to be seen.

We waited, a little stunned by the wasteland around us. A bell sounded across the water, faint, nothing special. We waited for it to sound again. Ten minutes—no bell. Twenty minutes—no bell. We stopped holding hands while I blew my nose.

"I wonder," Pookie said sadly, "if those two chickens are still in the can?" I frowned and said nothing, just stuffed the handkerchief back into my pocket. It never occurred to me what two chickens. We walked back toward the hotel and ate supper at the same drugstore where we had eaten lunch. Cokes and hamburgers again.

There finally came a moment in the evening when we were standing on the corner of Fifty-Seventh Street and Ninth Avenue, and we couldn't make up our minds if we should cross, go sideways, or backwards, or what. So we stood there silently during three or four light changes. Then, looking straight at the blinking "Don't Walk" signal, Pookie said, "It's all over, isn't it?" I said I guessed so. She turned her face up to me and her lips were trembling. She attempted a smile but her mouth couldn't quite make it. "Well..." she said, and then lost her composure and wiped her eyes with the cuffs of her sweater drawn tightly over her fists, and tried again, this time managing a smile. Her eyes in a few seconds had become red and puffed. "Well," she repeated, "bull-guano, five times nine."

That night we went to separate movies. Since mine let out earlier I was to leave the door open for Pookie. Which I did. She came back very late—it must have been about three in the morning—and sat down on the edge of the bed.

"You're awake, Jerry, aren't you?"

I hadn't yet gone to sleep.

"You want some barbecued chicken? I got it from a deli over on Ninth, and I can't eat it all."

I accepted the greasy bag wordlessly. She crossed the room, silhouetting herself in the window.

"I met a guy in a bar and told him what a bastard you were," she said listlessly. I waited for her to tell me that afterwards she had gone to his flat, but she didn't: she said; "It took a long time."

"Yes..."

She turned around and faced the bed—dark, featureless.

"I'm probably going to spend the rest of my life talking to people in bars, people on the other sides of counters, and people on buses, aren't I?"

"I don't know, Pooks..."

"Do you think if I really save twenty-one champagne corks, someone will marry me?"

I shrugged, a motion she probably couldn't see. "Pooks..."

"I know...I know. I'm going to wash my face and hands, comb my hair, and change into my pajamas and forget it..."

But she wouldn't get into bed with me. I said then she could have the bed alone and I would take the floor. But no, she didn't want the bed, she would take the floor. We had a minor argument over that. I admonished her to at least take the bed while I gnawed on the chicken. She wouldn't hear of it. She stayed in the desk chair while I put away the bird, then, too tired to argue further, I washed my hands and took the bed.

Pookie stationed herself on the floor, her arms folded on the edge of the bed, her chin resting on her arms. I lay on my back and stared at the ceiling.

"I'll pay for the pillow," she said softly.

"They probably won't even charge us," I replied.

"They cleaned it up nicely..."

"Yes..."

And there was no more to say. Silence settled. Occasionally I turned my head and found her eyes wide open staring at me. Maybe an hour, maybe a minute passed, then she put her hand lightly on my arm, and soon fell asleep. Myself, I couldn't sleep a wink. I was afraid to move for fear of waking Pookie up, yet I wished there were some way I could get her onto the bed without disturbing her. I found a feather in her hair and carefully plucked it out, and then I closed my eyes, and a long stream of Pookies crossed my inner eyelids: Pookies

[199]

balancing precariously on their toes, waving goodbye; Pookies drawing Long-Billed Sneets in the dust; Pookies dancing ahead with their arms flung gracefully out like wings; Pookies in the snow; Pookies in the moonlight; Pookies with their soft squinty eyes blinking out blurriness; naked Pookies turning around in little circles like windup toys; unhappy Pookies crying dimly in feathery snowfalls...

I opened my eyes and watched dawn come slowly into the room, first a grey light that took all color from everything, then a clearer light, then the sun. Pookie awoke with the sun and took her hand quickly off my arm.

She said; "Holy mackerel, am I ever stiff! What the hell did you let me do that for? Boy, does my mouth ever need a wash, and do my legs ever need a shave!" Grabbing her clothes, she bolted into the bathroom where she spent a good hour repairing whatever damage the night had done.

The first thing she said on coming out was: "I'm not going back to school today, I'm going home. For good."

And that was decided upon.

CHAPTER TEN

Right from the beginning, say you are brought by someone—your family, for instance—and you take a seat on the platform side, well—you spend fifteen excruciatingly foolish silent minutes in the throes of goodbyes."

We were in a taxi going down to Grand Central, and Pookie was giving me a long spiel on how she hated train rides.

"You know how it is," she continued. "You sit down, magazines on your lap, you look out, Mom waves, you smile, she smiles, Dad waves, smiles, Mom waves again, starts in on sign language you don't understand, Dad repeats very carefully what Mom is saying, you shake your head and mouth the words Blast off, will you? but of course they don't get it, the train jerks, creaks, everybody waves energetically, the train leaps forward and lays an egg, stops, hisses, and there you are again, facing each other, puzzled, and you begin to hate them for painfully doing what they believe is their painful duty... Then when the train is finally moving, I look out the window on a curve and see the engine maybe half a mile ahead, and I feel very far away from the heart of things.

[201]

I know it's stupid, but the idea of being tugged just never appealed to me."

This nervous condemnation of trains lasted all the way to the station. Being a Sunday morning, there weren't many travelers inside. "Like the first Sunday after a war," Pookie said. "All the people have been thinned out."

She went on to tell me while we were getting her ticket that one of her dreams was to walk into a very crowded station some day with a machine gun and let everybody have it. She liked the idea of herself, skirt uplifted daintily, stepping over a rug of bloody bodies burping occasionally, sending honey-colored bubblish souls up toward the smoky ceiling. Her chatter came out double its normal speed.

As it turned out, there was a westward bound train, but not for over an hour. So, after buying Pookie's ticket we plunked our suitcases down by the main information booth and prepared to glumly sit out the hour. She went off once to buy some magazines, and came back with everything from *Time* through *True Romance* to *Archie* comic books.

"While we wait, let's have a contest," Pookie suggested. "Give me all your pennies."

We pooled our resources and came up with twelve cents. Pookie scattered the pennies on the floor a short ways away from us. "We'll give a dollar to whoever picks them up," she said, taking the last one out of her billfold. When I realized that was all the money she had left, I offered to loan her some money, but she refused; she didn't want even a smidgin of a tie left with me when her train pulled out of the station.

Believe it or not, we waited a long time for someone to rise to the bait. A lot of people stopped to give the pennies the once-over suspiciously, but they all moved on. At long last a bald little fat man wearing a pin-stripe double-breasted suit stooped and began to laboriously pick them up. Here's the strange part, though: he picked up six pennies, straightened, adjusted his lapels, glanced both ways like in a gangster movie, and walked hurriedly away. We had to run to catch up with him.

"Congratulations, sir; you've just won a dollar!" Pookie boomed in a distraught M.C. voice, shoving the bill into the man's hand.

"I've just won a dollar? Why I just won a dollar?" I believe he was scared.

"You picked up those pennies, didn't you?"

His face lit up. "Yeah. I pick them up. Yeah, that's what I done. I pick them up." He opened his hand and demonstrated the six copper coins.

"Only tell me, sir," Pookie said; "why did you only pick up six?"

"Why only six...?" He scratched his head. "That's a good question, now I think about it. Why only six? I don't really know, I couldn't tell you. I'm there, see, bending over, picking up them pennies when I thinks to myself 'This is stupid, what I doing this for?' so I stand up. And I win a dollar, you say? How about that? Come to think of it, them pennies laying there like they was, well, it look like a kind of a trap..."

Pookie shook his hand again, and I shook it for the first time, shrugging and nodding at Pookie so he wouldn't get the idea it had been any of my doing. We returned to our bags just as they were being made off with by a very small rat-faced man in a very long grubby overcoat. He claimed they were his bags, I claimed they were ours, and he said okay, he must have made a mistake.

"I think we're going to blow it yet," Pookie said, as we straddled the bags for dear life. "I bet the ceiling's going to cave in any minute now. Or else a locomotive's brakes will fail and it will come plowing through the lobby right in a line with where we're sitting."

Suddenly I was so tired I could hold my head up no longer. I closed my eyes and drifted into a sort of semi-consciousness, yet I could still hear every word she said to me during that last half hour, and she said a lot.

First she described how her journey home was going to be. In the beginning she would be alone in a seat with no one beside her but her yellow reflection in the window. Big fat bugs would be splatting against the window like snowflakes. She would be hungry the whole way, but would be very thankful she had no money as she hated Almond Joys and vapid orangeade, and considered it an outrage the prices you had to pay for such junk. Her stomach would stop complaining when it realized that her pocketbook, like itself, was also empty.

Later on, some old woman (hag, that is) would mysteriously appear beside her. They always did. And they were always eating apples, and they always had lousy teeth, so every time they took a bite they had to gnaw on the apple for an hour or more. They always persevered, though, and got crumbs of apple all over the flabby fronts of their outmoded sackish dresses, and in the end they got the apple eaten.

Once at Merritt, her father would come to meet her at the station, no questions asked, provided she called home.

He would be crotchetier than ever as it would probably be raining cats and dogs. There would follow the inevitable reallocation talks with both blithering parents and they'd decide working for Daddy's real estate business would do her lots of good, at least until she was ready to sludge back to college, which she would never be.

The rest of the time—summer, fall—she'd mope around the town and country muttering about the injustice of it all, and maybe the following spring she would one day buy some flowers and put them on Joe Grubner's grave. She didn't know, though. Probably all she'd do would be to tuck the flowers in the grass beside his headstone and leave, slightly embarrassed by the whole thing.

Her voice became faint and reached me from far away. "The trouble is," she said, "that all good things in life take place in a minute—I mean added up. A dream, Grandpa Adams, Glorious beetles, bathtubs, falling in love ... I bet at the end of seventy years, should you live so long, you can probably sit down in a chair gnawing on your old apple and figure it out. You spent thirty-five years sleeping, five years going to the bathroom, nineteen years doing some kind of work you hated, eight thousand seven hundred and fifty-nine hours on the telephone, fifty-nine minutes blinking your eyes ... and then there's that one minute—sixty seconds. Or maybe ... maybe you won't even have the minute: my parents will never have it, never even come close to it. They've always been caught not paying attention—them and the famous plowman in Brueghel's Icarus. That could well be my trouble, Jerry. Maybe I've always been caught not paying attention when I should have, and blinking too much in between ... aah, bullguano! Who cares?"

Then I heard her voice—almost lost in the distance—say; "This'll probably give me the old menstrosity three times in three weeks..." and then, "I talk so much they'll have to sew my lips shut to keep me quiet after I'm dead..." then, "pow, pow, pow, you're a refrigerator..." and finally, "well, sleep tight, scruffy old kid from Charlie Chaplin land; no where in particular, here I come..."

Then I saw her walking down a long slope of white sand carrying her small suitcase, heading toward some kind of shadow I could barely make out in the distance there was so much quiet waiting mist. And as I watched she broke into a sort of slow motion dance, leaping softly into the air, her one free arm flung gently outward like a long white wing, and, faintly faintly, I heard her laughter, and then *Rotten egg...Jerry Payne's a rotten egg...* "Hey!" I shouted after her; "hey, Pookie—how many?" But she never answered. She danced straight into the mist, into the shadow, and disappeared.

My suitcase tipped over landing me on the floor with a rude bump. And she was gone; she was really gone. I searched for her among the passing people a long dull moment. My bewildered gaze at last fell to the floor where it came upon the six other pennies—still there. Still there.

I picked them up, breathed deeply, and bought a ticket for school.

Early in the evening of that same day, back at the fraternity house once again, I was awakened from a light snooze by Schoons' heavy hand on my shoulder. He reeked of booze.

"Boomaga," he slurred, "it's finally happened."

"What has?"

"The nippers; I lost 'em. Gone. Forever. Ta tata ta."

I said, "Why don't you get the hell out of here and go clean up or something?"

"What are you—a christer?"

"I mean it, Schoons."

"I bet you don't even care about my teeth, do you?"

"I bet you're right."

He blinked and leaned over very close, his lips puckered, his eyes weighted by a frown. He held his breath, and his eyes were blank for a moment, then they focused, puzzled, as if in mine he had discovered a foreign, unidentifiable thing, and then, as he slowly emptied his lungs so that a thin stream of liquored air warmed my cheek, a look of hostile recognition came over his entire face.

"Okay," he said, straightening and backing away, making an awkward who-cares motion with his hand. "So don't feel sorry for me, Payne. Who gives a damn?" At the door he steadied himself against the jamb, and, waggling his finger at me, opened his mouth to speak, then decided against it, and with an extravagant snort of disgust, left me alone.

I sat up, feeling as if a great burden had been lifted from my shoulders, lit a cigarette, then crawled through a window onto the back porch roof. Alone, I pensively smoked the cigarette while dusk grew heavy and the stock car faded into the darkening field below. In the chewed-up grass not far from the car, there was a small flock of birds, field plovers, standing very still among the glittering pieces of glass, their mournful tremulous whistles sounding ghostily through the twilight, and I felt a choking up inside, thinking of Pookie still on the train she hated, big bugs splatting against the window, still going home.

But a few moments later when I lay back and closed out the stars, the emotion was nearly gone. I faintly heard Poopsick wailing to be let in the front door; then I went to sleep.

CHAPTER ELEVEN

ALMOST a year later to the day, the morning
before my comprehensive oral examination in biology,
I received word of Pookie in a short, rather pathetic note:

Dear Jerry,
I've got some sleeping pills on the desk in front of me,
had them for a long time, in fact, and I've finally decided
to take them, lock, stock, and barrel, so by the time you
get this, I'll be a crumbled cookie. This letter is, in effect,
my suicide note; I couldn't bear writing it to my bigluvulating parents, God bless 'em both, nor to Uncle Bob,
pain hurts him so. I don't expect you to do anything;
I just wanted to say goodbye to someone. And after all, I
never did in Grand Central that morning, you know. You
will think of me sometimes, won't you?

Belatedly goodbye,
Pookie

My immediate reaction was to write the *Merritt Gazette*
for copies of their first edition after the date of Pookie's
letter. But I thought better of it in the end: after all,
what was the good of knowing one way or the other?

Better to let the matter rest as I'm sure Pookie wanted it to: never knowing for sure, always curious, always wondering, and a little tempted to inquire.

For I like to think that perhaps one day in the far far future I will most assuredly hear that she did not take her life, and has now become a famous writer or movie actress, or the wife of a famous athlete, living the quotable life she mentioned to me on the day I fell in love with her ...

But still and always Pookie; forever telling her stories to strangers.